CRISIS!

It was part of Bryony's work as an occupational therapist to win the confidence of her patients, and it was a job that she enjoyed doing, but there were other patients to whom she could have given immense help – if only she could bring herself to do it. It would mean reliving the dreadful event that had changed her life and destroyed her romance with Dr Max Anderson – the violent experience that she had been doing her best to forget. Now Max had come back into her life. Would this be the spur she needed to unburden herself at last?

Crisis!

by

Sarah Franklin

Dales Large Print Books
Long Preston, North Yorkshire,
BD23 4ND, England.

British Library Cataloguing in Publication Data.

Franklin, Sarah
    Crisis!

    A catalogue record of this book is
    available from the British Library

    ISBN   1-84262-285-4 pbk

First published in Great Britain in 1987 by Mills & Boon Ltd.

Copyright © Sarah Franklin 1987

Cover illustration © Heslop by arrangement with
Allied Artists

The moral right of the author has been asserted

Published in Large Print 2004 by arrangement with
Sarah Franklin, care of Dorian Literary Agency

Dales Large Print is an imprint of Library Magna Books Ltd.

Printed and bound in Great Britain by
T.J. (International) Ltd., Cornwall, PL28 8RW

CHAPTER ONE

Bryony parked as close to the Crown Court as she could and turned to Peter with an encouraging smile. 'Well, this is it. How are you feeling?'

The boy brushed his fair hair back from his forehead in the way he always did when he was nervous, and summoned a tremulous smile. 'I'm OK – be better when it's over, though.'

Bryony patted his arm. 'Before you know it we'll be getting back into the car again. Then I'll take you for that Big Mac I promised you.' She got out of the car and went round to the back to unlock the tailgate, reaching inside for Peter's folding wheelchair.

He had been paralysed from the waist down ever since he had been the victim of a mugging on his way home from the cinema eighteen months ago. His assailant had been caught after a string of other such attacks, and now at last he was being brought to justice. Peter, as the only victim who had been able to give the police a detailed description of the man's appearance, had been called as chief witness for the prosecution.

Working with paraplegics like Peter was part of Bryony's work as an occupational therapist, but, for reasons of her own, she found herself identifying strongly with his particular case. He was the first crime victim she had come across in her first qualified year. His parents, like hers, were both dead, and now his future had been tragically wrecked by the mindless attack that had also robbed him of the use of his legs.

But Bryony put aside her anger as she helped the disabled teenager into his wheelchair. It was her day off, but she had found it impossible to refuse when Peter had hesitantly asked her to go with him to court. Bill Kershore, the social worker in charge of his rehabilitation, had assured her that there was no need for her to give up her free time, but Bryony had insisted that she had nothing else planned for that day and would like to help. Neither Bill nor Peter could know, of course, about the memories Peter's experience had evoked for her; the deep traumatic hurt and the anger that such cases would never fail to rekindle. These feelings were locked deep inside – shared with no one. No one would *ever* know now, Bryony reflected as she wheeled Peter's chair up the ramp and into the court building. The episode that had changed her whole life was past history now. The secret was hers, to live with as best she could, though it would constantly chafe like a stone in the shoe of her subconscious for the rest of her life. All she could hope to do was to help others in similar circumstances back towards something resembling a normal life.

Bryony had been a qualified occupational therapist for a year now. In a strange way it had been the most rewarding year of her life; therapeutic for her as well as for her patients. During that year she had begun to learn not to look back – not to compare her life as it was now with the way it had been before. It took courage to rehabilitate oneself – more courage than most people realised, and she could well imagine what Peter must be going through at the prospect of seeing his assailant face to face across the courtroom this morning.

The waiting area of the court building was full of people, noise and bustle and, enquiring on her way in, Bryony had discovered that there might be a lengthy wait. She found a quiet corner for Peter's chair and asked him if he would like a cup of coffee.

He shrugged. 'Might as well, I suppose. It'll help to pass the time.'

She went in search of the drinks dispenser the attendant had told her about. As she fed coins into the machine and waited for the plastic cups to fill she wished as fervently as Peter did that the ordeal could soon be over. When she had promised to come with him to the Crown Court she hadn't realised how tense the atmosphere would be or how strongly she would relate to it. At that precise moment she could happily have turned tail and run – but she couldn't. She was here to support Peter.

As she made her way back towards the waiting area with the coffee a court attendant stopped her.

'Excuse me, miss. You're with the young man in the wheelchair – right?'

'That's right.'

He cleared his throat. 'Er – is he able to walk at all?' He glanced hesitantly over his shoulder towards where Peter was sitting.

'No – his attacker saw to that. He did a very thorough job!' Bryony bit her lip. She hadn't meant to sound so strident. After all, she wasn't here to involve herself in Peter's case, much as she would like to.

The man looked at her. 'Are you his nurse?'

'No, I'm – just a friend. He has no family, so I'm here to help and support him in any way I can,' she told him. 'Will I be allowed in there with him?' She nodded her head in the direction of the double doors leading to the court, her heart jumping a little at the prospect.

The man shook his head. 'I'm afraid not, miss, but don't worry, I'll take care of him. He'll be allowed to give his evidence from his chair. You can sit in the public gallery if you wish. The stairs are along there and to the left.' He pointed.

When she returned with the coffee Peter looked pleased to see her and drank it gratefully. 'Ever been to one of these places before?' he asked, looking at her over the rim of his beaker.

Bryony shook her head. 'Never.' *But I should have been,* an inner voice chided her. *Somewhere out there a man is walking free – free to damage and destroy, to wreck other lives, and all because I did nothing to stop him.*

'Are you all right? You've gone very pale, Bryony.' Peter was peering anxiously into

13

her face.

With an effort she pulled herself together and tossed back the last of her coffee. She was supposed to be here to support Peter, not to worry him! 'I'm fine,' she said, forcing a smile. 'Look, the attendant tells me you'll be able to give evidence from your chair. It seems I won't be allowed into court with you. But he says I can sit up in the public gallery, so I won't be far away.' She touched his hand. 'You'll be all right, love, won't you?'

He smiled bravely. ''Course I will.'

They both looked up as the usher called his name: 'Peter Gardner! Mr Peter Gardner!'

Bryony stood up as the attendant came forward to wheel Peter into court. She gave the boy's shoulder a reassuring squeeze. 'See you later. Good luck!' And without waiting she made her way quickly towards the staircase leading to the public gallery.

It was fairly crowded, and as she picked her way towards one of the few empty seats it occurred to her to wonder if all these people were in some way connected with the case being tried, or whether they were just sensation-seekers – people with a morbid turn of mind who revelled in the misfortune of others. Settling herself in the front row of the gallery, she looked down on the scene beneath her. Below, the court was set out in the traditional way, the judge in his red robe and wig presiding over the black-robed barristers and assisting legal executives; the court ushers and clerks. The accused stood in the dock. He looked normal and ordinary – frighteningly so – just like… Bryony averted her gaze. Inside, her heart was beginning to pound and her stomach churned sickeningly. She should not have come here today. Everything about this place was like a stick relentlessly churning the mud at the bottom of a pond. It was almost too much to bear.

Taking a deep breath to quell the nausea that rose in her throat, she glanced swiftly along the crowded row in which she sat, hoping she would be able to escape if necessary without making too much of a stir. Then suddenly her quickened heartbeat almost stopped with shock. At the other end of the row sat two men. As she looked, the one furthest from her turned to speak to his companion and for a second she found herself looking straight into a face she had almost convinced herself she had forgotten. But the strong, firm jawline, the dark, expressive eyes and thick brown hair, would be etched on her memory for as long as she lived. Blind panic rose suffocatingly in her breast. She had to get out of here before she made a fool of herself. She got up and began to make her way unsteadily towards the exit, muttering apologies as she fell over feet; oblivious to the muttered complaints as she stepped on toes in her panic-stricken haste. The counsel for the defence had already begun to examine Peter and people frowned, making *shhh-ing* sounds as she stumbled towards the door at the back.

Finding the safe haven of the Ladies, Bryony breathed deeply, fighting down the stifling panic. Max – Dr Max Anderson. Her lips formed the name experimentally. It was so long since she had said it. What a fool she was! There was no way the man in the gallery could have been Max. It must have been her imagination playing its old tricks. In the early days, when she had first come to Bridgehurst, she had seen him everywhere she looked. She had lost count the times when a deep voice, a dark head carried at that certain angle – a whiff of the aftershave he used, would quicken her heartbeat, convincing her that she had caught a glimpse of her ex-fiancé. But as the months passed, the imagined sightings had become fewer. She was over it. Or she had thought she was.

She took a deep breath and looked at herself in the mirror. A small oval face looked back at her out of large frightened dark eyes. 'You're weak!' she scolded herself. 'And despicable! You ran out on Peter just when he needed to know you were there. God knows what mincemeat that counsel is making of him!' Her hand still trembling, she took out a comb and ran it through her short dark hair, adding a dash of lipstick to her pale lips. She peered at herself again, angrily pinching colour into her ashen cheeks. 'You look like the clown you are,' she told herself, swallowing the knot of tears in her throat. 'No guts, that's your trouble! Get back out there this minute! If Peter comes out and you're not there waiting for him you don't deserve the privilege of calling yourself his friend!' And with this last piece of self-admonishment she picked up her handbag and walked back to the waiting room, her legs still far from steady.

Seating herself on one of the benches against the wall, she picked up a newspaper someone had left lying there. Glancing at the date, she saw that it was May the eighth. An

17

ironic coincidence. This very date four years ago should have been her wedding anniversary – the day she would have married Max. Everything had been arranged – the church, the reception at his father's house; the tiny flat they were to have shared, close to St Hildred's, a busy new hospital on the outskirts of the quaint Norfolk town where they were both working, Bryony as a student nurse in her final year, Max as a junior registrar, with Mr Jonathan Keller, the general surgeon. Their future had been assured. Not a cloud on the horizon. *Happy ever after,* Bryony told herself bitterly, throwing down the paper.

She swallowed hard. It was so long since she had allowed her mind to drift in this direction, but now it all came back in minute detail, as clear as though it were a video film, stored away faithfully in the dark recesses of her mind; the dress that had hung in her wardrobe, its delicate, simple beauty protected by a polythene shroud. The ivory lace lined with whispering taffeta had fitted her to perfection, clinging smoothly to her tiny waist and slim hips to flow out into a graceful flare... She closed her eyes tightly, trying to shut out the unwanted images; barely conscious of the

18

way her hands clenched into fists. It was over long ago – ruined and spoiled and *over!* It was months since she'd thought about it – cried over it, so why start again now?

She had often wondered if she might run into Max some day. In her mind she had planned what she would do and say. She'd honestly thought that by now she'd be able to handle it – yet the sight of that man up in the gallery, a face so uncannily like Max's, had thrown her into this wild panic. The shell she had built up over the last four years to shield her from the traumatic memories dissolved like mist, allowing her a glimpse back into the past she had fought so hard to forget.

It had been just a month before the wedding. She and Max hadn't been getting along too well. For weeks they'd been bickering about stupid things. Bryony had closed her mind to it, putting it down to pre-wedding nerves. Everyone seemed to have them. Everything will be all right once we're married, she'd told herself over and over. Everyone says so.

But it had come to a head with the idea for a weekend trip to Scotland. Max's father had insisted that it would do them both good to get away from all the wedding preparations for a couple of days, before the summer season got under way. He had even recommended a little inn just outside Fort William where he often stayed himself on fishing trips. It was all discussed and planned one night over dinner at the Andersons' house, while Bryony sat there feeling more and more resentful because she hadn't been consulted. Sitting at the dinner table with Max's father and aunt making plans over her head, she felt almost as though the trip was no concern of hers. She might not even have been present.

Max's father, Dr James Anderson, was the senior GP at the local health centre. He was also the local police surgeon. A large, blunt Scotsman, he took pride in calling a spade a spade, and his sister Louise, who had looked after her brother and his son ever since Max's mother had died, had the same uncompromising nature.

Later, as they were drinking their coffee, the talk turned to the recent spate of violent crime that had broken out in the district, and the direction the conversation had taken had irked Bryony into an even more resentful state of mind.

'Well, I blame all these violent television

plays and films,' Lou Anderson had announced in her usual forthright manner.

'Oh, I think it goes a little deeper than that, Lou,' Max's father said mildly. 'I remember watching quite violent gangster films and Westerns when I was a laddie, and *I* never wanted to go out and mug some poor body in the street afterwards.'

Aunt Lou sniffed. 'Things were different in those days. You and I were brought up with discipline and a sense of right and wrong, James.' She shook her head. 'Nowadays the young have no respect for anyone or anything. And as for these girls – they *ask* for all they get, if you want to know what I think!' she said. 'The clothes they wear, for a start!'

'Surely a woman should be able to go out into the street wearing whatever she chooses without the fear of being attacked?' Bryony said hotly.

Max touched her hand under the table, giving it a warning squeeze, but she ignored it. Aunt Lou was always throwing out snide hints about what she wore. She seemed to have a deep-seated antagonism towards modern youth and labelled the young unreservedly as everything from irrespon-sible to plain criminal. Bryony was getting sick and tired of it.

Louise Anderson went on, ignoring Bryony's defensive remark, 'Skin-tight jeans – necklines almost down to the waist, topless sunbathing. No shame at all! Then when they get attacked they wonder why!' She gave a snort of mirthless laughter as she looked round the table. 'Ask James if you don't believe me. He's often said that ninety per cent of all rape cases are the girls' own fault.'

James Anderson's colour deepened as he looked up sharply at his sister. 'Oh, come now, Lou. I've never said that and you know it.'

'Maybe not in so many words, but you meant it,' said Aunt Lou, wagging an unrepentant finger. 'I haven't lived with you for twenty years without knowing how your mind works.'

Under the table Max felt Bryony's hand stiffen in his and rose hastily to his feet. 'I think I'd better be getting Bryony back to the nurses' home,' he announced. 'She's on early duty in the morning, aren't you, darling?'

Bryony opened her mouth and then closed it again. Max was right, of course. However strong her views it would not be politic to quarrel with Aunt Lou at this particular moment in time. As Bryony had no mother of her own Max's aunt was arranging the whole wedding herself, even down to doing all the catering, a fact of which Bryony found herself constantly reminded as the date drew closer. As Max drove her home that evening she remarked on it to him.

'I wish your Aunt Lou hadn't taken everything on herself. I wish we could just run off somewhere and get married without all the fuss,' she sighed.

Max glanced at her. 'Oh, she's not such a bad sort, you know, and she's loving every minute of it. She's never had any children of her own, remember. She's devoted most of her life to Dad and me. And now you'll be the nearest she's ever had to a daughter.'

And she's going to get plenty of mileage out of that too, by the look of things! Bryony told herself silently. 'Nevertheless I think we could have managed to organise our own weekend trip,' she told him. 'To hear her this evening no one would think *I* had anything to do with it at all! She and your father don't seem to have given a thought to the fact that I've got my finals coming up in just a few months. I really need all the spare time I can get for studying.'

Max drew the car off the road and switched off the engine. 'Darling, I'm sure no one meant to leave you out of anything. And you know a couple of days' break will help you to unwind from the tension of studying so hard. You'll pass your finals, I'm sure of it.' He kissed her gently on the forehead. 'Anyway, I'm the one you're going with, not Dad or Aunt Lou.' His eyes laughed into hers as he drew her close. 'And they haven't really organised the trip at all, you know. *I* have.' He smiled at her. 'Want to hear *my* plans?' She relaxed in his arms, laying her head against his shoulder as he said: 'For starters we won't be staying at the Mackenzie Arms.'

Bryony twisted her head to look up at him. 'We won't?'

He shook his head. 'I've already booked a room for us at another little hotel in the next glen.'

As the words sank in she looked up at him enquiringly. 'Did you say *room?*'

He nodded. 'Of course.'

Bryony sighed. 'Oh, Max...'

He held her away from him and looked into her eyes. 'For heaven's sake, Bry – we'll be married in a month's time!'

She pulled away from him to sit upright

again. 'I know. That's it – that's *why*...' She broke off awkwardly, shaking her head. 'We've waited this long. I wanted everything to be perfect.'

Max drew a deep breath. 'It will be. Darling, you know as well as I do that we've only waited this long because we've hardly had any choice,' he reminded her. 'With you sharing a room at the nurses' home and me living at home we've had hardly any time alone together at all – that's why I thought this weekend would be a chance to relax together.' He looked into her eyes. 'Darling, can't you see – this is the reason we've been getting so edgy with each other... Oh, *hell!*' Seeing her withdrawn expression, he removed his arm from her shoulders to clamp his hands over the steering wheel, his eyes staring angrily straight ahead and his mouth set in a tense, hard line. 'Honestly, Bry, the way you go on to poor Aunt Lou about modern, liberated young womanhood! If only she knew what a *phoney* you were. I feel like assuring her that she's got nothing to fear where you're concerned!'

The harsh remark cut her deeply and Bryony sat staring miserably down at the clenched hands that lay in her lap. 'I wish you'd try to understand. There's more to being liberated than sleeping around.'

Max sighed impatiently. 'I'm not asking you to sleep *around,* Bryony. Though if that's the way you see it – as something *sordid*...'

'Oh, Max, it isn't that I don't want to...'

'Then what *is* it, for God's sake?' he demanded crossly.

She shrugged, at a loss. 'It would spoil everything. I'd feel so furtive signing in with different names,' she told him lamely, unable to express what she really felt on the subject.

'As if anyone cares! Anyway, what's to stop us signing in under the same name? After all, what's the difference – a month from now...'

'Exactly – a *month,* so why can't we just wait? Please try to see it my way, Max.' She turned large, darkly appealing eyes towards him, knowing she hadn't a hope of making him understand. She sighed. Surely they should be able to talk freely. If she couldn't make him see that romantic idealism was her only motive for wanting to wait, what hope had they of making a successful marriage? But she could see by his face that it was no use. He was determined to misunderstand. He seemed to take a certain

26

delight in making her out to be prudish and cold, which was about as far from the truth as it could be.

A lump thickened her throat as Max switched on the ignition and revved the car engine noisily, betraying his irritation. 'All right,' he said tightly. 'You win. Perhaps the idea of spending a weekend away from it all isn't such a good idea after all. Maybe we'd better call the whole thing off!'

They parted coolly and Bryony lay awake all that night, worrying about the future. She had been trying for weeks to convince herself that it was pre-wedding nerves, coupled with anxiety about her looming finals, that was causing all the trouble between them, but now she had to face facts. What Max had said this evening had been true: with neither of them having the privacy of a flat or even a room in which they could be alone they had had no opportunity to allow their feelings for each other full rein; in fact she had begun to wonder lately just how well they knew each other. This evening's disagreement was just another to add to a list of many. It seemed lately that she and Max disagreed on almost everything, and the thought frightened her. She turned restlessly in bed, trying desperately to reassure herself that everything would magically come right after the wedding; that as long as they loved each other...

For most of that night she tossed and turned endlessly, her mind tortured by doubts. She loved Max so much. The memory of his hurt, angry reaction to her refusal to share a room wounded her to the heart. Perhaps she was wrong to cling to her silly romantic ideals. The thought of losing him filled her with despair. She longed to be his wife – so why couldn't she convince him of the fact?

Several days went by before Bryony saw Max again, mainly because she was on night duty in Accident and Emergency while he was working in the daytime. Apart from fleeting glimpses in the hospital corridors, they had little contact with each other, and in the brief moments when they did meet the weekend trip wasn't mentioned.

In the early hours of Friday morning a man came into A and E supporting another whose face and clothes were spattered with blood. When Bryony had cleaned him up it was clear that the man had sustained some very nasty facial lacerations that looked suspiciously as though they had been caused by a broken bottle. Even after the patient's wounds had been dressed and he had been admitted for observation his friend stayed on, hanging around in the waiting area, watching Bryony in a way that made her feel edgy. Finally she went across and advised him to go home.

'You won't be allowed up to the ward at this hour to see your friend,' she told him. 'Better to go home and get some rest. I imagine he'll be allowed home tomorrow after the doctor has seen him. If you'd like to telephone we'll let you know.'

'When do you go off duty?' the man asked with a leer.

Bryony shook her head. She and the other nurses on A and E were used to this kind of thing and had learned how to cope with it. She made a lighthearted remark about nurses never going off duty and went back to her duties. Next time she looked she was relieved to see that the man had taken her advice and left. It wasn't an unusual incident. At the weekends there were often drunks in A and E. Occasionally they had to call the security officer to deal with obstreperous cases, but to her relief the man went away without further incident, and Bryony thought no more of it.

It was just before the shift ended that Sister Johnson came looking for her. Bryony had just come back from X-Ray with a milkman who had been brought in after dropping a full crate on his foot. It had been a hectic night, and she quickly smothered a yawn when she saw Sister waiting for her just outside her office.

'Oh, there you are, Nurse Slade. There was a telephone call for you.'

'Oh. Who was it?' asked Bryony.

'Dr Anderson, as a matter of fact,' Sister said, her grey eyes twinkling. 'He asked me to give you a message. He'll meet you at the main gates when you go off duty.' She glanced at her watch. 'Might as well start tidying up ready for the morning shift now. It's pretty quiet at last, thank goodness.'

'Thanks, Sister. I'll make a start.' Immediately Bryony's feeling of lethargy left her and she was wide awake. Max wanted to see her! Maybe they could still go away for the weekend. She would tell him she was sorry – they would be able to talk, make up their quarrel. Right away from here, from his father and Aunt Lou, everything would be all right.

Bryony could hardly wait for the shift to be over. As soon as the new shift took over she grabbed her cape and shoulder bag and set off towards the main gates, taking the short cut through the wooded grounds. It was quiet, hardly a soul about at this hour, and she breathed in the fresh pine-scented early morning air gratefully, enjoying the birdsong that later would be drowned by the roar of traffic on the busy road outside the gates.

She had just crossed the doctors' car park when she heard soft footsteps behind her. A voice called: 'Excuse me, Nurse, can you tell me the way to Outpatients, please?'

She turned. 'Yes. You're going the wrong way...' With a small start of surprise she recognised the man who had brought in the facial lacerations case earlier. 'Oh, it's *you* – what are you *doing?*...'

Without warning the man grasped her arm in a vice-like grip and pushed her into the dense shrubbery on the fringe of the car park. A large rough hand clamped itself over her mouth as she opened it to scream. She had read of many such attacks in the newspapers – often imagined what she would do in similar circumstances – little knowing how utterly defenceless she would be against such determined brute strength.

Long afterwards, when the shock had subsided, when the bruises had healed, it was the things he had said – the verbal attack, that lived on in her mind. The implication that it was all her fault, that she had in every way possible invited that attack. Her uniform, her provocative manner, her hair style, make-up… The hate on his face and his sadistic pleasure in hurting and degrading her were indelibly etched on her memory; scars that she was convinced would never ever fade.

It was late afternoon when Bryony arrived at her aunt's flat in Bridgehurst. She hardly remembered the journey, except that she had been glad of the drive – of something mechanical on which to concentrate her mind so that she couldn't think too much about what had happened.

Alison Slade was a mere twelve years older than her niece. She was a clinical psycho-logist, based at the busy City Hospital in Bridgehurst in the industrial Midlands. The two had been close ever since the death of Bryony's parents, and it was the most natural thing in the world that Bryony should go to her in trouble.

When she opened the door of her flat Alison had gasped with surprise. 'Bry! Darling, how lovely to see you, but to what do I owe…?' The smile faded from her face as she saw her niece's distressed expression. Already the tears were beginning to stream down her cheeks and her slight frame was trembling violently. Alison reached out a hand to guide her gently inside.

'Darling, what on earth is the matter? Is it Max? Has something gone wrong? Come in and tell me all about it.'

But it had taken a strong sedative and several hours of sleep before Bryony had been able to unleash the trauma that tormented her mind and body. Even then, although shocked and angry, Alison hadn't fully appreciated the true agony of the situation.

'You should have gone straight to the police,' she insisted. 'Maybe you still can. I'll drive you back to Woodchester right away. You do still have the clothes you were wearing, don't you?' she asked practically. 'They'll need them for forensic…'

'*No!*' Bryony shuddered violently. 'I can't go back there, Alison – please don't make me. I burned my uniform – everything, so there's no point.'

Alison stared at her. 'But you must! You can't let that – that *creature* get away with it!'

Bryony shook her head. 'Don't you see – if

I went to the police Max's father would know. He's the local police surgeon!'

Alison took her hands and held them tightly. 'Darling, listen to me. Of course I understand that it would be difficult for you, but it wasn't your fault. No one could possibly blame you. They'll have to know, anyway,' she went on gently. 'You can't face a thing like this by yourself. Max will need to know. He's your fiancé. You'll be married in a few weeks' time.'

'No!' Bryony sprang to her feet and began to walk restlessly up and down. 'I wrote Max a letter – one to my Senior Nursing Officer too. I've left St Hildred's – left Max. I can't ever go back there – I can't marry him now. Don't you see? I have to put it all behind me and make a new start, Alison. Please understand – *please help me!*'

CHAPTER TWO

'Are you sure you didn't want to wait for the verdict?' Bryony and Peter were seated in the seclusion of a corner table in the café where she had promised to take him after his court appearance. It was still quite early for lunch and they had the place almost to themselves.

He shook his head. 'No. I just wanted to get away as fast as I could. I hope I never have to go through anything like that again.' He looked at Bryony, his blue eyes hurt and puzzled. 'Why did that lawyer try to make out that I was lying? Did he think I planned to spend the rest of my life in this chair as some kind of – of *practical joke?*'

She smiled gently at him. 'They have to do it, Peter. It's their job,' she told him. 'Everyone is entitled to defence – it's the law. I'm sure no one really suspected you of lying.' But even as she spoke her heart went out to the frail-looking fair-haired lad in the wheelchair. The waitress placed two plates of hot food in front of them and Bryony smiled. 'Gosh, that looks good! Eat up and try to forget it now, eh?'

Peter nodded, applying himself to the food. As he ate he looked at her thoughtfully. 'Someone told me you used to be a nurse. Is that right?'

She nodded. 'That was a long time ago.'

'What made you give it up?' he asked.

'That's rather a long story,' she told him evasively. 'I decided that nursing wasn't for me and came here to live with my aunt. She's a clinical psychologist at the City Hospital and she suggested that occupational therapy might suit me better, so I decided to train for that. It turned out to be the right decision. I was able to train here in Bridgehurst and I often work quite closely with my aunt, which is nice.'

'Didn't you feel all that other training was a waste of time, though?' asked Peter.

She shook her head. 'Oh no. My nursing experience was a great help, actually, so the three years I spent doing that haven't been wasted at all.' She smiled. 'It's a fascinating and rewarding job. I get to move around and meet a lot of interesting people – like you.'

Peter's pale cheeks turned pink. 'I don't see how anyone can see me as interesting.'

36

He looked at her shyly. 'Thanks for coming with me today, Bryony. You know, it wasn't a bit like I thought it was going to be. I wasn't exactly looking forward to it, but at least I thought I'd feel some kind of satisfaction, seeing him standing up there in the dock at last; getting what was coming to him.' He shook his head. 'I didn't, though. I just felt...' he frowned. 'It sounds funny but – well, sort of ashamed; as though I'd done something wrong!' He looked up at her, a perplexed expression on his young face. 'Can you understand that?'

'I can,' Bryony told him softly. 'Oh yes, I can.'

By the time she had returned Peter safely to the rehabilitation centre where he was living, Bryony found she hadn't an ounce of energy left. The day had taken an enormous emotional toll of her, leaving her feeling limp and exhausted. Back at the flat she still shared with Alison she took a leisurely shower and then set about preparing the evening meal. She was in the kitchen when her aunt arrived, calling out as she always did, the moment the door had closed behind her:

'Hello! I'm home.' Alison opened the

kitchen door and dropped her briefcase on to a chair, sniffing, as she began to take off her outdoor things.

'Mmm, that smells good. I'm starving – didn't have time to stop for lunch.'

Bryony turned from the cooker. 'Do you *ever*? It's no wonder you're so thin!' She took in her aunt's tall elegant figure and shining chestnut hair, thinking not for the first time that she looked more like a model than a lady who spent her life studying disturbed minds. She looked at least ten years younger than her thirty-six years. Bryony always marvelled at Alison's calm, relaxed manner – a quality that she herself had had good reason to be thankful for many times during the past four years.

'Hurry up and wash if you're going to,' she chided, smiling. 'I haven't slaved over a hot stove for hours to have it going cold!'

'How did it go today?' asked Alison ten minutes later as they sat down to eat.

Bryony told her aunt about Peter's ordeal and how he hadn't stayed to hear the verdict. 'I expect it'll be reported in the local papers,' she concluded. 'Poor boy, I really felt for him.'

Alison looked up sharply at the tone of her niece's voice and asked: 'Were you in court?'

Bryony swallowed hard. 'No. Well, yes, I did go into the public gallery, but I – oh, I don't know.'

Alison peered closely at her. 'Did something happen? Did you find it upsetting?'

Bryony shook her head. 'Not really – well, a bit...' She laid down her knife and fork. 'Alison, something *did* happen, actually. I wasn't going to mention it, but – I thought I saw Max.'

'I see.' There was a slight pause, though Alison's expression didn't change. 'So you ran away?'

Bryony winced at her aunt's bluntness. Alison believed in looking life in the face and had no time for beating about the bush. 'Yes,' she admitted, 'I'm afraid that's what it amounted to. And I'm not exactly proud of myself, so you needn't look at me like that,' she added defensively. 'After all this time it was quite a shock. I thought I'd stopped seeing Max's face everywhere I looked a long time ago.'

Alison took a forkful of food and chewed thoughtfully before replying. 'As a matter of fact, it might easily have *been* Max,' she said at last.

Bryony's eyes widened as she stared at her aunt. '*What!* what do you mean?'

'I've been meaning to tell you – waiting for the right moment,' Alison confessed. 'This seems to be as good as any.' She looked Bryony straight in the eyes. 'Max started a GP course at the City Hospital last week,' she confided. 'I hear he's making a special study of forensics, is running a course in forensics to run alongside it and apparently Max is doing that too. It seems he's planning to take over from his father when he retires – both in the practice and as police surgeon.'

Bryony was listening in shocked silence, trying to absorb the information. 'I see. So you've seen him – spoken to him?' she said at last.

Alison shook her head. 'Good heavens, no! I don't even know if we'd recognise each other. After all, we only met the once. That little scenario came to me via the hospital grapevine – you know how news spreads at the City.' She glanced anxiously at her niece, wondering just what effect all this was having on her. For all her experience in the field of psychology she still found it impossible to assess Bryony's emotions as fully as she would have liked. Since those early days when it had been possible to help her over the storms of weeping that alternated with moods of seething, frustrated anger, Bryony had developed a disquieting way of clamming up that often left Alison feeling at a loss. She knew only too well that her niece still suffered from the memory of her attack, and she seemed to have developed a way of submerging her feelings; a fact that worried her aunt.

Alison tried to sound matter-of-fact as she went on: 'That's why I said you may well have seen Max this morning. I daresay it's inevitable that part of the course will include spending some time in court.'

Bryony gave up all pretence of eating and laid down her knife and fork, pushing aside her barely touched plate. Her mouth was dry as she said: 'This is an unexpected development. What do I do now, Alison?'

The older woman sighed. 'Look, love. I don't think it would hurt you to confide in me more. I don't like to push you, but it doesn't do to bottle things up, you know.' She paused before asking quietly: 'Just how do you feel about Max now?'

Bryony shrugged, her eyes clouding again. 'It was all over four years ago. You know that.'

Alison sighed. Here it was again: the stone wall. 'So you've always persisted in saying,'

41

she said bluntly. 'But I only know what you tell me. I'm still not clear why. I've never understood why you felt unable to go to him after what happened that morning.' Bryony remained silent and Alison shook her head. 'I've tried not to probe, love, but there must have been something sadly amiss with your relationship if you had so little faith in him.'

But Bryony's mind was buzzing with the kind of confusion she thought she had done with for good. How could she make *anyone* understand that it was herself she had lost faith in on that beautiful spring morning four years ago? The cruel, sadistic attack on her mind and body was relatively brief, but its effect was as painful as ever. Self-doubt had eroded her confidence, made her unsure of all the things she had taken for granted – her femininity, her suitability for nursing, ever her status as a human being, but perhaps the guilt she felt was worse. She should have reported the attack, she knew that only too well. It would have been so easy. Someone who knew his identity lay close at hand in a hospital bed – the accident victim he himself had brought into A and E. Because of her cowardice another girl might have been attacked – a child, even! It was something she had had to live with, but it had taken its toll, changed her; made her feel unworthy and second-rate. She had shied away from making her humiliation public knowledge – and more especially from having Max and his family know. Even after all this time Louise Anderson's disapproving remarks still echoed in the dark corners of her mind. *They ask for all they get. They bring it on themselves!* Was it possible? *Could* she have unwittingly invited the attack – in spite of herself? It was so long since she had allowed her mind to stray along this track, and she shuddered involuntarily, knowing without a shadow of doubt that facing Max again would be an ordeal.

'Bryony! Did you hear what I said?' Alison's voice was sharp as she leaned across the table towards her. 'I hope you're not going to let this spoil all you've built up for yourself. You've done so well. You have a real gift for occupational therapy and you have a very bright future ahead of you if you approach it in the right way. It would be very wrong to contemplate running away again. Surely you and Max can meet on friendly terms – find some common ground by now?' She glanced thoughtfully at her niece. 'Just what *did* you say in the letter you left him, anyway?'

Bryony dragged her thoughts back to the present. 'Very little. Just that I felt we were unsuited – didn't know one another well enough. After all, we'd only known each other a few months.' She took a deep breath and looked her aunt in the eye. 'I told him I'd changed my mind – that it would never have worked between us – that he wasn't to try looking for me, because I wouldn't go back.'

'In other words, you jilted him!' Alison said bluntly. She reached across the table to cup her niece's chin, forcing her to meet her eyes. '*I* can understand why you did it, but he can hardly be expected to, especially when you never paid him the courtesy of telling him the truth. Did you ever try to put yourself in his place? Can you imagine how he must have felt?'

Bryony pulled away from her aunt's firm hand. 'Don't! I couldn't tell him – couldn't tell *anyone,* let alone Max.' She frowned, shaking her head impatiently. 'Let it rest now, Alison. It's over and done with – past history.'

But Alison wasn't quite finished. 'Tell me one thing, Bryony,' she persisted, 'were you ever really in love with him?'

Bryony felt her heart lurch painfully.

44

Swallowing hard, she said: 'Of course I was. But there were – problems, even before – before what happened. What I wrote in that letter wasn't entirely untrue. Max never really understood me. Maybe we hadn't had time to get to know one another. Maybe we were too young.' She shrugged. 'Anyway, I daresay he's married by now. The grapevine told you so much, I'm surprised they haven't got his marital status on record too!' She managed to laugh and Alison allowed herself to relax a little.

'Well, in that case it's simply a matter of getting that awkward first meeting over,' she said. 'And if you ask me, the sooner it's over and done with, the happier you'll be.'

Bryony stood up and began to clear away the plates. 'I wouldn't bet on it,' she said under her breath.

As she got ready for bed that night, Bryony looked at herself in the mirror over her dressing table. Fleetingly she wondered if it had been Max in court this morning and, if it was, had he seen *her?* If he had, why hadn't he reacted? But as she examined her reflection now, the answer was clear. She'd changed. She had changed her appearance quite deliberately after coming here to

45

Bridgehurst. The long, dark hair, once worn in a smooth chignon when in uniform and tumbling free about her shoulders when she was off duty, was now cut in a short crisp style which was less feminine and more businesslike. It suited her elfin face, giving her an almost boyish appearance. In the old days she had worn soft pink lipsticks, mascara and eye-shadow to enhance her large dark eyes. Now she hardly ever used make-up. She had changed her style of dress too; abandoning the soft feminine styles and colours she had once liked in favour of muted shades and plain classic lines. Subconsciously she did her best to merge into the background as much as possible.

For the first time in months she allowed herself to think about Max. Lying there as sleeplessly as on those terrifying nights in the months following the attack, she allowed him once more into her mind. What had happened to him over the past four years? *Would* they meet? The City Hospital was vast, and anyway, Bryony spent most of her time outside it. Months could go by before it happened. Maybe he would even pass her in the street without recognising her. She told herself that she hoped so – and almost – *almost* managed to believe it.

Fenning House was a residential rehabilitation centre for the physically handicapped. It housed a dozen or so people of varying ages in bright, attractive bed-sitting rooms, supervised by Pam and George Browning, who, along with their two young children, lived in the adjoining warden's house. Ten o'clock the following morning saw Bryony arriving on her weekly visit. Each patient received her individual attention with the guidance of his or her doctor, but Bryony conducted group sessions too, in the specially equipped kitchen where the patients would learn to cook and clean with the specially adapted gadgets, the aim being to teach them to become self-reliant so that they could eventually live alone again.

As she drank coffee with Pam and George she checked on the various patients' progress.

'Peter has seemed rather down since the court case yesterday,' Pam remarked. 'I'm afraid it rather seems to have set him back. I've been wondering if I should ask his doctor to have a look at him.'

Bryony sighed. 'I was afraid of that. It's only natural that he should have been upset, but he wouldn't even stay to hear the verdict.'

George looked up angrily. 'Maybe it's just as well. I don't know if you've heard, but that thug got a two-year suspended sentence. His counsel managed to convince the judge that he was a reformed character. He pleaded that the attacks were carried out because of severe depression due to his being un-employed. He's since managed to get a job on an oil rig which he would lose if he went to prison – so...' He threw up his hands in exasperation. 'It makes me see red to think that he's earning good money while poor Peter will be in that damned chair for the rest of his life – lucky to earn *anything!*'

Pam put a steadying hand on his shoulder. 'Nothing we can do about it, love. Our job is to help pick up the pieces. It wouldn't do to let Peter catch your mood either.'

George nodded, smiling at Bryony apologetically. 'I know. It's just that it seems so bloody unfair – the injustice of it.' He stood up, his normally cheery smile firmly back in place. 'Right, shall we go, then?'

The morning session in the kitchen went well, though Bryony was a little disturbed to find that Peter didn't appear. Asking one of the care assistants, she learned that he was feeling tired and spending the morning in bed, and as soon as she had seen the others settled with the coffee and biscuits they had made themselves, she put two cups of coffee on a tray and carried it along the corridor to Peter's room. Tapping softly on the door in case he was sleeping, she received a subdued: 'Come in.'

Opening the door, she looked round it to find the boy propped up in bed, an unopened book lying on the bed-tray in front of him.

'Hi,' she said with a smile. 'We all missed you, so I thought I'd bring my coffee in here and have it with you.' She looked at him enquiringly. 'If you feel like a chat, that is. If you'd rather be alone, just say and I'll understand.'

Peter smiled. 'You always do understand, Bryony. Of course I'd like a chat. Thanks for the coffee too.'

She put the tray down and pulled up a chair. 'Listen, Peter, I'm going to try something new later this week – something I went on a course for a few weeks ago. I'd like your advice on it.'

Peter's depressed expression began to brighten. 'What is it?'

'Drama – remedial drama, to give it the full title.'

His jaw dropped a little. 'Acting, you mean?'

'That's right. What do you think?'

He shook his head. 'Surely it'd be a bit limited – with us the way we are?'

'Not at all. That's just the point. I think – *know* it's great fun and very good therapy. What I'd like you to do is to persuade as many of the others as you can to attend, because of course it'll be an optional session.'

The boy perked up visibly. 'OK, just you leave it to me. I'll get them there. When is it?'

'Well, I thought...' Bryony got no further. At that moment the door opened and George looked in.

'Peter, Dr Capes is here to see you.'

Bryony stood as the middle-aged GP walked into the room. The doctor smiled at her and then at his patient. 'Good morning, Miss Slade. Sorry to interrupt. Now then, young man, I've brought another doctor along to see you this morning. He was in court yesterday during your case and has asked to meet you.'

He stood aside to reveal a younger man, tall and broad-shouldered, who walked smilingly into the room holding out a hand to the boy in the bed.

Dr Capes smiled at Bryony and stood

back. 'Dr Anderson, this is Miss Slade, our occupational therapist. She does a great job for the patients here.'

Max Anderson turned his head sharply to look at the girl almost hidden by the half open door. Taken off guard, his dark eyes widened incredulously for a moment as they met hers. But his reaction was only momentary. Recovering instantly, he said calmly: 'Miss Slade and I have met before.' He held out his hand, looking straight into her eyes. 'How are you?'

Bryony's mouth dried and her heart seemed to stop beating at the sudden shock of coming face to face with Max. He looked older – a different man almost. There was a new gauntness about his face. The jaw seemed squarer – the cheekbones more pronounced; his mouth looked harder and firmer. She noticed too, with a small shock, that there were even a few threads of silver in the thick, dark wings of hair brushed back above his ears. She cleared her throat, and her lips felt stiff as she uttered the usual polite noises. Reluctantly and briefly she put her hand into his, withdrawing it quickly – hoping he wouldn't notice how cold and clammy it was.

She could feel her colour rising as she

backed towards the door. Excusing herself, she promised Peter hurriedly that she would see him again soon. Her legs felt like jelly as she closed the door behind her. Leaning briefly against the wall of the corridor for a moment to recover, she took a deep breath. So that was it! That first dreaded meeting was over. Although it had lasted only a few seconds it had been even worse than she had visualised. Max, on the other hand, had seemed totally unruffled; barely surprised even. Only one thing had emerged from the meeting: it was clear that he had put their broken engagement behind him long ago. To him it was obviously very firmly in the past and no longer aroused feelings of any kind for him.

What had he been thinking as they faced each other? Perhaps he was reflecting that he had had a lucky escape? Whatever her reason at the time, perhaps she had done the right thing in leaving him, she told herself – for both their sakes.

CHAPTER THREE

Work on the children's ward at the City Hospital was something Bryony looked forward to. It was such a joy to see so many small faces smiling up at her when she entered the ward for her weekly session with them. But even the children couldn't cheer her out of her bleak mood the following morning. However, she adjusted her smile and tried hard to forget her own problems as she guided them into the various creative pursuits to which they all looked forward so eagerly.

When the less handicapped of her patients had been started on their painting and handicrafts Bryony moved on to the weekly session of teaching the more severely disabled children to use the specially designed gadgets that would make their future lives easier, painstakingly helping them to re-learn the skills of feeding and dressing themselves, a task that needed endless patience on the part of both patient and therapist.

While she worked that morning Bryony had noticed a little boy lying quietly in one corner of the ward. She recognised the telltale symptoms of hydrocephalitis and asked the staff nurse about him.

'His name's Nigel and he was admitted last week with suspected meningitis,' Jane Fairman told her. 'Luckily it turned out to be a mild viral strain, so it wasn't as serious as it might have been. He was in intensive care for a few days, but he's done so well that Mr Galbraith has allowed him to be moved down here. He thought being among the other children might help to arouse some interest in his surroundings.'

'And has it?' asked Bryony.

Jane shook her head. 'Not so far. You can't even get him to look at you.'

Bryony moved across to the cot and looked down at the pathetic little boy. Reaching out, she touched his hand, but he shrank from her as though her fingers burned him. 'Does anybody try to talk to him – get him to react?' she asked quietly.

Jane sighed. 'We've tried, but you can see what happens. He shrinks away, like a little sea anemone – closing up when anyone approaches him.'

Bryony shook her head. 'Maybe I can get

54

his interest.' Fetching a box from her case, she opened it and took out some smooth pebbles, putting one of them into the child's hand. He dropped it immediately, staring into space with no change in his vacant, blue-eyed stare. Bryony tried again with a seashell, but there was still no response. Then she had an idea: in the box were some empty eggshells, salvaged from the breakfast table. She took one and pressed it between Nigel's two hands. As he felt the crisp, crunchy feel and heard its sound a flicker of interest twitched at his facial muscles. A smile lifted the corners of his mouth and the blue eyes blinked and looked momentarily into Bryony's brown ones.

'Feels good, eh, Nigel?' She smiled at him, placing a fresh shell between his hands and pressing again. 'See – it's fun, isn't it?'

Staff Nurse Jane Fairman beamed with delight. 'That's terrific! The first time he's shown any interest in anything since we've had him here.'

'Keep on trying with tactile objects,' Bryony advised. 'Next time I come in I'll try to remember to bring more textures to stimulate his senses. Who knows, we may even get him to join in the games, with luck.' She looked at her watch. 'Heavens, look at the time! I've got some house calls to make and I'm running late. Better start clearing up.'

Jane smiled. 'I'll help you.'

As they worked Bryony thought Jane looked slightly preoccupied, and at last she asked her if there was anything wrong. The other girl sighed.

'I had some news last night. My flatmate is getting married.' She glanced up at Bryony. 'I'm pleased for her, of course. She was over the moon. The trouble is, I can't see how I'll be able to afford the rent on my own. It's such a pity, it's a really nice flat.' She gave Bryony a rueful smile. 'Just when I thought I'd said goodbye to the nurses' home for good, too.'

'Oh dear.' Bryony tidied the last paintbox into her case and snapped it shut. 'But you'll find someone else to share with, won't you? I daresay you'll have plenty of time to ask around.'

But Jane shook her head doubtfully. 'Not really. The wedding isn't for a couple of months yet, but the thing is, they've found a house they like and they want to move in at once. As Sheila pointed out, it seems daft for them to go on paying rent when they'll already be paying a mortgage. They have acres of decorating to do too. I can see their point. It's the logical thing to do.'

Bryony looked thoughtfully at the other girl. 'Not very romantic, though.'

Jane shrugged. 'Who's romantic nowadays? Practicality wins every time!'

Bryony was silent for a moment. 'I suppose I've always had old-fashioned ideas about that sort of thing,' she said, half to herself. 'White weddings – honeymoons – making vows and keeping them. It's the kind of thing you don't mention any more for fear of being laughed at.'

Jane grinned ruefully. 'Join the club,' she whispered. 'I feel the same way. It comes of reading too many romantic novels, I suppose. But don't tell anyone I said so!'

Bryony smiled. 'Try not to worry. I'm sure you'll find another flatmate. Surely there are plenty of people who would jump at the chance of sharing a nice flat like yours.'

Jane shook her head. 'Maybe, but Sheila and I got along so well. Jumping at the first person who came along could be disastrous. Maybe I'm a bit set in my ways, but I couldn't bear the idea of someone who left the kitchen in a state and a ring round the bath.'

Bryony laughed. 'I know what you mean.'

57

She picked up her case. 'Well, the best of luck. Let me know how you get on.' She said goodbye to the children and was walking down the corridor, her mind full of what Jane had been telling her, when the lift at the end of the corridor wheezed to a halt and the doors opened to emit a group of white-coated doctors. Suddenly she became aware of a familiar voice, and froze. Any second she was about to come face to face with Max again. Looking around for some way of escape, she stepped into a recessed ward entrance and flattened herself against the wall, crossing her fingers that the group were not paying a visit to this particular ward. To her immense relief they passed without noticing her, still talking. Max's broad, white-clad shoulder passed within inches of where she stood, his deep voice making some remark about community care. She was just breathing a sigh of relief when the ward door opened and a surprised voice addressed her from behind.

'Bry Slade, as I live and breathe!' A cheery face topped by a thatch of thick sandy hair confronted her as she spun round. Geoff Mason, the physiotherapist, grinned at her warmly. 'What are you doing, lurking in the doorway like that – loitering with intent?'

'Oh – Geoff, it's you.' Bryony raised an involuntary hand to her throat.

He peered at her, frowning. 'What's up, love? You look as though you've just seen a ghost!'

'I have,' she muttered. 'It's nothing – someone I didn't want to see, that's all.'

He nodded. 'Oh-oh – in debt again, eh? Or is it your guilty past catching up on you?'

'What do you mean by that?' she asked sharply – too sharply. Geoff's face fell. He was only joking. The remark was typical of him, but it had caught her on the raw. 'Sorry, Geoff,' she muttered, colouring. 'I'm a bit on edge this morning.'

'You can say that again!' Dropping an arm across her shoulders, he walked along the corridor with her. 'And I'd like to know why.' He glanced at his watch. 'Got time for coffee and a natter?'

She shook her head. 'Sorry, I only wish I had, but I'm running late as it is.'

As they reached the lift he drew her round to face him. 'You're not yourself, sweetie, are you? In fact you look positively peaky to me. Look, let me buy you dinner tonight, then you can tell your old Uncle Geoff all about it. If you absolutely have to I might even let you have a little weep on my shoulder. What about it, eh?'

Bryony chewed her lip. 'Well – I don't know...' The lift doors opened and three people got out. She looked at Geoff. 'Are you going down too?'

'No, up. I'm on my way to Men's Surgical. You'll come tonight, then? Pick you up at eight.' And before she could think of an excuse he pushed her firmly into the lift. As the gap between the closing doors narrowed she saw his infectious grin widen as he waggled his fingers at her. 'By-ee!'

So she had a date with Geoff? Maybe it would be nice to go out with him. They had worked together on a good many cases and he was the only man she knew that she felt relaxed with. His powerful shoulders and tough physio's build belied the gentle nature and kind, sympathetic heart that she had come to know and trust over the past months. Besides, she was almost certain that Geoff Mason wasn't interested in her as a woman, but merely – and comfortingly – as a friend.

The first of Bryony's housecalls that morning was to an elderly man who had had a stroke and lost the use of his right arm and hand. He had been suffering from severe depression, refusing to take an interest in anything, and Bryony had been almost at her wits' end until, quite by accident, she had learned that before his illness he had been a keen amateur artist. She had enlisted the help of Mike Davis, a retired art teacher who had sometimes helped her with difficult cases in the past. For the past two weeks he had been helping Mr Grimshaw to learn to paint with his left hand, and this morning Bryony was looking forward to finding out how they had been getting along.

When she arrived at the neat terraced house on the outskirts of Bridgehurst she found his wife looking a lot happier and less harassed than of late. As they stood in the narrow hallway she told Bryony in a hushed undertone that her husband and his new friend Mike 'hit it off a treat'. 'I haven't seen him so cheerful for a long time,' she said, holding out her hand for Bryony's coat. 'But I daresay he'll grumble just the same. You mustn't take any notice of him. He's much more cheerful, take my word for it. Go on in. I'll make the coffee now you're here. Kettle's boiling.'

Mr Grimshaw sat in his favourite chair by the window, his useless right hand lying limply on his knee. He was looking out at the neat pocket-handkerchief-sized garden he loved.

Bryony smiled at him. 'Good morning, Mr Grimshaw. How are you this morning?'

He turned to her, pulling down the corners of his mouth. 'Just look at all those damned weeds out there. If I could just get *at* them...'

'Keep up with your physio and you will!' Bryony told him cheerfully. 'Now, what about the art lessons?'

Mr Grimshaw couldn't quite stop the corners of his mouth from lifting. 'Ah well – never occurred to me to try to use the left hand, did it? If it had...'

'Am I going to be allowed a peep at your work?' asked Bryony with a sideways smile at his wife as she came into the room with a tray of coffee.

'You are *not!* At least, not yet.' Mr Grimshaw flexed his left hand. 'You can as soon as I get used to doing everything the opposite way round – and get this hand more supple; I'm doing exercises for that, you know – that young Mason is giving me some; as well as the ones for my leg.'

'That's great!' Bryony told him. 'I shall expect to have my portrait painted before the year is out.' She sat down and leaned across to touch the old man's hand. 'There's no reason why you shouldn't get a lot of the use back in your right limbs, you know. And won't it be useful to be able to do things with either hand? You'll have the advantage of us all!'

As Mrs Grimshaw saw her out a little later she laid a hand on her arm. 'Thanks for all you're doing for Bob,' she said softly. 'You and Mr Davis and young Geoff – you're all so helpful. I don't know what we'd have done without you.'

As Bryony got into her car she remembered her aunt's words. Occupational therapy certainly fulfilled her more than nursing had. She had made a wise choice. Briefly she allowed herself to wonder what kind of life she would have been living now if things had been different – if she had carried on nursing and married Max – if she hadn't been on duty in A and E that morning – if... Quickly she turned the key in the ignition and put the car into first gear. Sometimes it didn't do to speculate on what might have been.

When Alison heard that Bryony was going out with Geoff that evening she had been pleased. 'Do you good!' she announced. 'You haven't been out for weeks. I've warned you often enough, you're going to get square eyes looking at that television!'

Bryony laughed. 'I do other things too, you know – like preparing work and studying patients' case notes.'

'You can have too much of that too,' said Alison. 'A girl of your age needs to break out occasionally and do something frivolous.' She smiled. 'Geoff's just the man for you in your present mood!'

Sitting back in the passenger seat of Geoff's bright red sports car later, Bryony tried hard to relax. She hoped he wouldn't ask her too many questions about who she had been trying to avoid this morning. She was rather taken aback to discover that he had booked for the Friday dinner dance at the Country Club on the outskirts of town.

'I hope you approve.' He cocked an enquiring eyebrow at her. 'There aren't many of these old-fashioned places around any more. I thought you'd like it.'

Bryony laughed. 'I *think* that's a compliment! Anyhow, I shall take it as one.'

'Oh, it is – it *is!*' Geoff ushered her solicitously to the bar and ordered the drinks. But as soon as they had consulted the menu and ordered he launched straight into the subject she had been dreading.

'Right – give.' He leaned forward eagerly

on his bar stool.

'Give what?' said Bryony, trying to look puzzled.

'Oh, come on! You know what I'm talking about. This morning – who were you hiding from – who was it you didn't want to see?'

'Oh, that!' Bryony toyed with the stem of her glass, avoiding his eyes as she searched her mind for an explanation she thought he would swallow.

He cocked an eyebrow at her. 'By the way you're hesitating I'd hazard a guess that it's got something to do with a past love affair – right?'

She gave up. 'All right – yes. Satisfied?'

He looked outraged. 'I most certainly am *not!* You're supposed to be here for the express purpose of unburdening yourself.' He searched her eyes. 'You can trust me, can't you, Bry?'

She sighed impatiently. 'Yes, Geoff, of course I can. I'd just prefer not to talk about it, that's all.'

'Oh – I see. I'm sorry, I didn't mean to pry, just wanted to help.' He looked hurt and she immediately regretted her brusque tone.

The waiter arrived to tell them that their table was ready, and when they were seated on the red velvet banquette at a secluded corner table, Bryony looked at Geoff. 'It's simply this, Geoff: the man I was once engaged to has just started a GP course at the City Hospital,' she told him quietly. 'It's rather an uncomfortable situation. I keep bumping into him – or rather trying to avoid it.'

'I see.' He nodded understandingly. 'Awkward. How long since it ended?'

'Four years – a bit more,' she told him.

His eyebrows rose. 'Oh, well, if it's that long surely you can iron things out by now,' he suggested. 'Establish a truce if not a friendship?'

She sighed. 'I don't think so. You see, I ran out on him just a few weeks before the wedding.'

He stared at her with wide eyes as the waiter put their starters in front of them; barely able to contain himself until the man had gone. 'You mean you jilted him? *Wow!* Why, Bryony? It must have been something pretty bad for you to do that.'

Inwardly she groaned. She might have known that Geoff wouldn't easily let the subject drop. 'Let's just say it seemed like the only thing to do at the time,' she said evasively. 'Now, can we talk about something more cheerful, please?' She tucked into her avocado vinaigrette and changed the subject briskly. 'Mmm, this is very good! It was a stroke of genius, finding this place, Geoff. I do like it.'

To her relief Geoff took the hint and began on his own starter, launching after a moment or two into an amusing account of the harrowing problems he and his flatmate Paul had been encountering lately with their landlord. Paul was a keen classical music buff and had just invested in an expensive stereo system. Their landlord was rather less than enthusiastic about it, though, and had been complaining about the noise.

'You should have seen Paul's face when the old chap told him to turn down *that row!* He went quite purple. I thought he was going to have a fit!'

Bryony laughed, picturing the elegant Paul's indignant face at hearing his beloved music described so irreverently. She was feeling much more relaxed now and was beginning to be glad she had come.

After the dessert Geoff looked at her enquiringly. 'This group's quite good, isn't it? It's a nice change from the eternal disco. Want to dance?'

She reached for her bag. 'I think I'd like to

go and tidy up first,' she told him. 'I'm sure that creamy concoction has demolished most of my lipstick. Shan't be a minute.'

In the ladies she repaired her make-up and flicked a comb through her hair, reflecting as she regarded herself in the mirror that it was marvellous how a couple of glasses of wine could relax one. Maybe Alison was right – perhaps she should do this more often. Geoff might show rather more interest in her private life than was comfortable at times, but his heart was in the right place and he did make her laugh. As she made her way back across the restaurant the floor was quite crowded with couples dancing. As she caught a glimpse of their table through the throng she could see that Geoff was talking to a good-looking redhead whom she recognised as Sara Daneman, the newly qualified doctor daughter of Dr Daneman, the City Hospital's senior pathologist. But it was only when Bryony actually reached their table that she saw that the girl was not alone. Opposite her, on the banquette she herself had vacated, sat a man, presumably Sara's escort.

Even though his back was towards her, Bryony recognised him immediately and her heart plummeted. Her first panic-stricken instinct was to turn and run, but it was too late, Geoff had already spotted her.

'Oh, there you are! I'm sure you must have met Sara Daneman. She's in her pre-Reg year on Mr Galbraith's firm. And this...' he looked across at the tall dark man opposite, 'is Dr Anderson. Have I got it right?'

'Max, please.'

He was smiling at Geoff, but as he turned his head and caught sight of Bryony his smile faded abruptly.

Geoff prattled on: 'This is Bryony Slade, my favourite occupational therapist.'

Sara smiled. 'Hello, Bryony. Haven't seen you for ages.' She looked at Geoff. 'Before we go, have that dance with me, Geoff. There's something I want to talk to you about. You don't mind, do you?' She glanced briefly at Bryony and Max, then grasped Geoff's hand and led him towards the dance floor.

Slowly and shakily, Bryony sat down, looking tentatively at Max. 'How are you?' she asked politely.

'I'm very well, thank you.' His voice sounded as cold and brittle as ice. A waiter passed and he raised his hand. 'Would you bring me a Scotch and soda, please?' He glanced at Bryony. 'Something for you?'

69

'No, thank you. Are you enjoying your course?'

'Very much.' He seemed intent on watching the dancers.

She chewed the inside of her lip, squirming inwardly with embarrassment. 'Is your father well?' she asked. 'And your aunt?'

The waiter brought Max's drink and he downed almost all of it in one go, then met her eyes directly and suddenly in a way that took her breath away. 'Listen, Bryony. I may as well come to the point: I won't pretend I wasn't dismayed at finding you here. In fact shocked would be a better word. But there's nothing either of us can do about it, so we must put up with it. The point I'm trying to make is that I'm here to work and I don't intend to let anything – or *anyone* – get in the way – understand?' He fixed her with eyes of granite and she felt her throat thicken as she replied quietly:

'I've no wish to make things awkward for you, Max. I never wanted that.'

'Didn't you? Well, you could certainly have fooled me,' he told her, a bitter edge to his voice.

'Naturally I wouldn't deliberately embarrass you,' she went on. 'No one here – except my aunt Alison – knows of the connection between us, and no one need.'

'Thank you,' he said stiffly. 'That is the way I'd prefer it.' Without actually saying so he managed to convey the impression that he would infinitely have preferred never to have set eyes on her again, and she cringed inwardly at the blistering hostility in his eyes and tone of voice.

When she saw Geoff and Sara coming back to the table she felt weak with relief. Smiling up at them, she asked: 'Enjoy your dance?'

'Very much,' said Sara. 'Now it's your turn!' When neither Bryony nor Max moved she urged them: 'Go on! I'm still trying to persuade Geoff to join in my charity walk next month.' She grinned gleefully at a cowering Geoff. 'A fraction more arm twisting and I'll have him!' She gave Max a pointed look. 'Go *on*, darling. I'm sure you'd like to dance with Bryony, wouldn't you?'

He finished his drink and stood up with obvious reluctance, looking at Bryony with a frosty smile. 'Will you?'

She mumbled something incoherent and rose, walking ahead of him to the small floor on legs that felt too feeble to support her. At that moment she would have welcomed earthquake, flood or fire; anything to have escaped those searing eyes and the ordeal of dancing with him.

But she was unprepared for the effect the feel of his arm about her waist would have on her; the cool hand lightly holding hers or the close proximity of his face. The spicy scent of his aftershave brought back heart-achingly evocative memories, and she swallowed hard, wishing Geoff could have chosen anywhere else but this place to have brought her this evening.

As they circled the floor the silence between them developed the tension of a violin string till Bryony could bear it no longer. 'Have you known Sara long?' she asked Max.

He answered without looking at her: 'About a year. Our fathers are old friends from college days.'

'I see. How nice.'

'She's a talented girl – very ambitious – hoping to take her Fellowship eventually and become a consultant.'

'I know.' She permitted herself a sideways glance at him. 'And you? I thought you had plans in that direction too.'

There was a small silence before he replied: 'I learned long ago that it isn't wise to look too far ahead. Sometimes the priorities shift, as I'm sure you appreciate, Bryony. Dad will be retiring in a few years. I've always known he cherished hopes that I'd take over from him when the time came.' He shrugged. 'Police surgeons need to be a little more clued up on pathology and forensics nowadays. That's basically why I'm here.'

The point of his remarks hadn't escaped her, but she kept her voice light as she said: 'I see. It must be very interesting.'

'It is.'

Bryony longed to return to their table. Max was clearly as unhappy in this situation as she was. But the music seemed as though it would never end. She racked her brain for something else to say, but as she opened her mouth to begin Max spoke too.

'I...'

'The new...'

She shook her head, laughing nervously. 'Sorry – what were you going to say?'

'I was just remarking that the new idea the police have of opening up their centre at the City Hospital is a good one.'

Bryony frowned. 'I'm sorry, I don't seem to have heard of that.'

'Really? It's a revolutionary new idea for victims of violence – female victims.' He turned to look at her. 'In other words, a rape crisis centre.'

The words seemed to explode inside her head like bullets and Bryony closed her eyes as the room seemed to spin out of control, quickening her heart and taking her breath away. She felt Max's arm tighten around her and heard the concern in his voice as he asked:

'Bryony, what's the matter? What is it?'

She tried to take a deep breath, praying that she wasn't going to faint and make a fool of herself, but the spinning room, Max's face and the other dancers seemed to dissolve into a mist as her legs buckled beneath her.

CHAPTER FOUR

'But why didn't you *warn* me?' Bryony sat opposite her aunt, facing her accusingly. After her apparent collapse at the Country Club Geoff had brought her home. He had been full of concern, fussing all the way until she could have screamed with irritation. Alison had tactfully packed him off home, assuring him that Bryony had been working much too hard and would be fine after a rest. Now the two women faced each other across a tray of Alison's special strong coffee.

'I saw no need. The centre's not even open yet.' Alison avoided her niece's eyes as she poured the coffee. 'They're converting the old short-stay wards. We need a larger S.S department now that anaesthetics are so much better. More and more ops nowadays need only a short...'

'But you never even mentioned it!' Bryony interrupted. 'Yet you of all people must have been in on it from the very beginning – *why?*'

Alison returned her gaze with frank blue

eyes. 'Why do you think?' she challenged.

'You thought the idea might upset me?' Bryony shook her head. 'For heaven's sake, Alison! It's four years now. You don't have to tread on eggshells with me any more.' But she couldn't quite get the conviction she'd hoped for into her voice. She took a long drink of her coffee, wrapping her cold hands tightly round the cup. 'It was hearing it from Max that shook me,' she confessed. 'Hearing him say – that word. It was almost as though – as though somehow he *knew.*' She looked up, her lip trembling. 'You've no idea what an ordeal tonight was, Alison. And passing out like that!' She bit her lip hard. 'Heaven alone knows what he must have thought!'

Alison sighed. 'I can imagine how difficult it must have been for you, love. But there's nothing either of you can do about it. There's nothing to be achieved by agonising over it.' She spooned sugar into her coffee and stirred thoughtfully. 'Actually, Bryony, I was waiting for the right moment to tell you about this new idea for a special reason.' She looked up. 'It's something of an innovation. The police have asked the hospital authority to co-operate, providing a place where victims can be interviewed and examined in

76

pleasant surroundings so as to reduce the trauma; away from the environment of a police station. It's to have a different title too; a less dramatic one. It's to be called a Victims Examination Suite.'

Bryony nodded, resisting the urge to clamp her hands over her ears. 'I see.'

'And I was going to suggest that you might help,' Alison finished.

Bryony's eyes widened incredulously as she stared up at her aunt. *'Me?'*

'Yes.' Alison leaned forward. 'They're looking for volunteers – the right sort of volunteers; anyone who could share the burden in the initial stages. Just talk and listen. I think you'd be perfect. Personally, I feel there's probably a place for your skills as an OT in that field as well.'

Bryony's arms closed across her chest as though to protect herself; an unconscious gesture that didn't escape Alison's notice. 'I'm sorry, it's out of the question,' she said abruptly, shaking her head. 'If I'm directed there in the course of my job I shall have to do it, of course, but to ask me to volunteer...' She swallowed, glancing at her aunt. 'I'd be hopeless. Surely you can see that?'

'I don't agree. I think it would help you

too, Bryony,' Alison said quietly. 'You've never talked enough about your own ordeal – never truly got it out of your system. If you'd only...' She left the sentence unfinished, looking hopefully at her niece. 'Will you at least give it some thought?'

Bryony stood up, feeling suddenly stifled. The room seemed to have become too warm – too stuffy. She longed for a long hot bath and her bed. 'All right,' she said abruptly, 'I'll think about it. It's the one thing I try *not* to do, but if you insist...' She walked to the door, looking back at her aunt, her hand on the handle. 'But I can't do more than think, so don't expect anything.'

Much later, as she lay curled into a tight ball, staring into the darkness, hot tears stung her cheeks. Would it be like this for the rest of her life? Would there always be something to remind her – rearing an ugly head when she least expected it, like a spectre; reawakening all the nightmare memories? No one – *no one* understood. Even Alison with all her training and experience couldn't know how she felt. Closing her eyes, she saw Max's face, the iciness in his eyes when he spoke to her. He hated her, despised her for what he thought she had done to him. Resentment made her clench her fists tightly under the bedclothes. She had wounded his pride, his precious pride. If only she could tell him that wounded pride was nothing compared with what she had suffered – that to her the whole world had been plunged into bleak and bitter darkness that morning as he had waited for her at the hospital gates.

'I'll put it behind me if it takes forever,' she promised herself, her lips moving silently as she framed the words. 'I'll throw myself into my work. At least no one can take that away from me!'

Bryony's first remedial drama session at Fenning House on the following Monday morning was greeted with an unenthusiastic reception. Peter Gardner had kept his promise to talk to his fellow patients about it, but in the main they viewed the idea with scepticism. Only four people including Peter gathered in the recreation room on Monday morning. But Bryony was prepared for this. The tutor on the course she had attended had warned them that the attitude of most disabled people was initially scathing and pessimistic. She had sensed a slight ripple of interest as she plugged in her tape recorder, though, and an increase in curiosity when she fetched a bucket of water and some other items from the kitchen; leaving their use deliberately unexplained.

She gathered them into a circle and drew up her own chair. 'I think Peter has been telling you that we're going to do some drama,' she said brightly, looking round at the four faces. Their expressions varied between embarrassment and blatant disbelief. Kathy Marshall, a middle-aged accident victim, spoke up, her tone challenging:

'Think you're going to make film stars of us, do you?'

Dave Freeman, a young man a little older than Peter, added his view. 'I'll tell you straight, Miss Slade, I'm only here because Peter asked me to come. It's bad enough being tied to this chair without having my limitations shoved down my throat. Acting – I ask you! What will they think of next?'

Bryony's confidence began to slip slightly. It was one thing hearing all the theories on the course, quite another being faced with three hostile and reluctant participants. However, she pressed on. Turning hopefully to the other member of the group, a beautiful young coloured girl, she asked: 'What about you, Leonie – why did you come?'

Leonie shrugged. 'I didn't have anything else to do!'

Bryony sighed inwardly. There didn't seem much to choose between hostility and apathy. Maybe she should have tried first with another group – children perhaps. She smiled at them brightly. 'You all like plays, don't you, the theatre – films – television?'

There was a grudging murmur of assent, then Leonie said: 'I like the soap operas best.' She turned to Kathy. 'Did you see that evening dress Sue-Ellen had on last week? It was really gorgeous. It was gold, with...'

'Bloody 'ell! If *this* is what it's going to be about I'm off.' Dave turned his wheelchair and headed for the door.

'Please don't go, Dave,' Bryony pleaded. 'At least not till you've told me what *you* like. This is a new experiment for all of us, remember. If you're going to write it off before you've given it a chance...'

Dave relented, coming slowly back into the centre of the room. 'Oh, all right, then. If you really want to know, I like a good thriller,' he offered.

Kathy giggled. 'Miss Marple?'

'No, not that silly old cow!' Dave scowled at her. 'More your James Bond.' He grinned. 'You know – some good car chases and a few tasty birds thrown in.'

'And spies,' Peter chimed in. 'And power-mad millionaires intent on conquering the world.'

Suddenly they were all talking at once, deep into a discussion on what each of them liked, until Leonie looked at Bryony and said: 'What's the use of all that, though? *We* couldn't act that kind of thing – not with all that action.'

'We *could!*' Bryony cut in. 'We could do it like a radio play – and even record it if you like, so the others could hear it.' She reached out to touch the tape recorder on the table beside her.

Her statement was received in stunned silence. For a moment she thought she was back to square one as they all stared at her. Then Dave suddenly grinned and said: 'OK then, great! What are we waiting for?'

After a shaky start the session went well. By the end of the morning they had worked out a story-line between them, decided who should play what parts and even experimented with sound effects, using the things Bryony had borrowed from the kitchen. Dave in particular proved specially inventive in this field and the session ended with all four participants looking forward eagerly to the next.

As Bryony packed up her things and prepared to leave Peter touched her arm. 'Can I have a word with you before you go, Bryony?' he asked shyly.

'Of course.' She looked at him closely. He wasn't so pale today, but there was a thoughtful look in his eyes. 'There's nothing wrong, I hope?'

He shook his head. 'No, I'm fine. Bill Kershore, my social worker, has been talking to me, though – about training for some kind of career.'

Bryony smiled. 'That's great, Peter. Have you decided what you want to do?'

He smiled wryly. 'It's not quite that easy. Let's face it, there isn't a lot of choice, is there – me being the way I am?' he ran a hand through his fair hair, looking up at her shyly. 'What makes it worse is that the thing I really want to do seems pretty unlikely, according to Bill.' He looked at her hesitantly, prompting her to ask:

'And what's that, Peter?'

'I want to be an occupational therapist – like you.'

'Oh! – I see.' Too late, she realised that she had hesitated just a fraction too long.

'You see – you think I'm mad too.' Peter

turned away. 'Bill's reaction was the same. I might as well have suggested volunteering for the next moon shot! Looks as if I'd better forget it.'

Bryony reached out to touch his shoulder. 'Don't jump to conclusions, Peter. It's just surprising to me that you should choose my job.'

'I've got enough O and A levels,' he told her. 'I've checked. And when you think about it, most of the places I'd have to work in would have facilities for a wheelchair, wouldn't they? It takes four years to train, I know, but that isn't a problem. Heaven knows I've got the time.' He studied her face, looking for the smallest sign of encouragement. 'I'd just passed my driving test before I was injured,' he added. 'I'm sure I could learn to manage an adapted car.'

The bright eagerness on his young face brought a tightness to Bryony's throat. She swallowed hard and forced a smile. It was flattering that she should have inspired Peter to try to train for her job. All the same, there was likely to be opposition to his choice. She only hoped he wouldn't be disappointed. 'I'll do what I can, Peter,' she promised. 'In the meantime speak to as many people as you can about it. You can't have enough people on your side.'

'I've already started,' he told her. 'I've already told Dr Capes about it. And Pam and George, of course.'

Bryony was preoccupied as she walked out to the car. There was no reason she could think of why Peter should not achieve his ambition. Many blind people trained for physiotherapy, and she had even heard of one man, badly burned, who so admired the plastic surgeon who had rebuilt his face that he went on to become a plastic surgeon himself. The more she thought about it, the more she felt she should take up Peter's cause.

'Hi there! Where have you been all weekend? My finger nearly dropped off dialling your number!'

Bryony turned to see Geoff walking towards her across the car park.

'Hello, Geoff. Alison and I were out most of the time. The weather was so nice.'

Geoff leaned an elbow on the roof of her car and looked at her quizzically. 'So – you were out enjoying yourself while there was I, worried stiff, imagining you lying limp and lifeless in some hospital bed! You might have let me know you were OK. You scared the daylights out of us all the other night, you know.'

Bryony smiled at his typical exaggeration. 'Don't over-dramatise. It was only a dizzy spell. Alison thinks I may be a bit anaemic.' She had tried her best to sound casual, but as she reached out to open the car door Geoff's hand descended to cover hers. Startled, she looked up at him.

'It was him, wasn't it?' he asked quietly. 'Dr Max Anderson.'

'W-What was?' she asked, her mouth dry.

'Come off it, Bry. What we were talking about earlier that evening. He was the man you jilted. I'm right, aren't I?' As she opened her mouth to protest he frowned and shook his head. 'I'm not thick, you know. It didn't take many two and twos to add up to that conclusion. You'd already said he was at the City on a GP course. You looked as white as death when you saw him, and then – when you passed out cold in his arms...'

'Geoff, if you mention a word of this to anyone else...' Bryony found herself trembling. 'If it gets around I shall have to give up my job and leave Bridgehurst. I'm not joking.'

He grasped her shoulders warmly. 'Hey, steady on! What do you take me for,

86

Bryony? I wouldn't do anything to hurt you, I'd have thought you'd know that by now. I was just concerned for you, that's all. I wanted you to know that I'm on your side, even though I don't know the facts. If you walked out on the guy, there must have been a damned good reason. That's good enough for me.'

Relief flooded through her and she smiled weakly up at him. 'Thanks, Geoff, you're a good friend. Max isn't an ogre. It's nothing like that.' She shook her head. She was getting into deep water again. 'I'd like to explain, but...'

He gave her shoulders a brief squeeze. 'No need, love. No need. Don't give it another thought.' He looked down at her. 'You're sure you're all right now?'

'Fine.'

'You wouldn't like me to sort anyone out for you?'

She smiled. 'No, really. I can handle it.'

'You're sure?'

'Quite sure.'

'That's all right then.' He smiled at her. 'So – on to important matters. When are we going out again?'

'I don't know. Give me a ring some time, eh?'

As she drove away from Fenning House Bryony was thoughtful. Now two people knew of the relationship between herself and Max. How long before others found out? Would Max tell anyone? Perhaps he had already told Sara. They certainly seemed close. Well, she would have to live with it, she told herself. And if everyone blamed her she would just have to survive that too. After all, guilt was no stranger to her!

Half of that afternoon was reserved for the monthly assessment meeting at the City Hospital when therapists, physicians and social workers met to compare notes about patients' progress. It was the time when suggestions were put forward and discussed, and Bryony had made up her mind to mention Peter's ambition to train for OT. She had spoken to Bill Kershore beforehand to sound out his feelings on the matter and found that they were the same as hers. Alison was at the meeting and so was Graham White, the occupational psychologist in charge of most of the patients at Fenning House. The last member of the group to arrive was Dr Capes, the GP. Bryony was rather surprised to see him there and even more surprised when Max followed him into the room to sit at his side. She acknowledged him briefly, then lowered her eyes to her case notes, wishing the warm colour she felt burning her cheeks would quickly subside.

The meeting followed the usual routine and went without a hitch until it came to Peter's case. Bill Kershore put forward the suggestion that Peter should be allowed to train for occupational therapy, and Bryony quickly endorsed the suggestion, adding that Peter was eminently suitable and that in her opinion any physical disability would be more than adequately compensated for by his enthusiasm and his sympathetic disposition. Here, Dr Capes, who had so far remained silent, spoke up.

'Actually the reason I am here today is to talk about this patient,' he said. 'Some of you may know that Peter Gardner had been experiencing a certain amount of spasm in his lower limbs. This in itself is not unusual, but Dr Anderson and I have examined him intensively and we're both of the opinion that he could possibly be helped by surgery. I've consulted Mr Grierson, the orthopaedic consultant, and he has agreed to examine the boy shortly. Obviously much will depend on the outcome of any possible treatment, so

I would suggest that you shelve any decision until a prognosis is made.'

Bryony looked at Bill. The two were silent, but Bryony was dismayed. Peter had been through so much already, both mentally and physically. Many paraplegics experienced the spasms Dr Capes had mentioned and their hopes were always raised by them. They hardly ever heralded any measure of recovery, so why should it be imagined that they would in this case? Raising her eyes, she saw Max looking at her and quickly looked away, feeling again the hated telltale colour creep into her cheeks.

A little later, on the way out of the building, she heard her name called and looked up to find Max hurrying down the steps towards her. Reluctantly, she waited for him to catch her up.

'Bryony, I meant to telephone after the other evening. Are you feeling better?'

'Yes, thank you. It was nothing – the room was rather hot. I don't usually faint.'

'As long as you're all right.'

'I am – thanks.' Was this why he had caught her up? She shifted her weight from one foot to the other, not quite sure how to bring the conversation to an end. 'Well, I...' she turned away.

'Can we have a word?' he asked.

She looked at him. 'Oh – yes. Perhaps we could be walking towards the car park. I still have a couple of calls to make.'

He fell into step beside her. 'I noticed that you seemed to doubt the wisdom of Dr Capes' suggestion about young Peter Gardner.'

She shrugged. 'I'm only an OT. It's not up to me to question a doctor's decision.'

'Nevertheless, it's understandable,' Max said reasonably. 'Peter's a very likeable lad and it's a sad case. Obviously you'll have had some experience of paraplegia and you'll know that spasms are not uncommon, but when I was on Jonathan Keller's firm at St Hildred's a couple of his patients made complete recoveries. He found that there was pressure on the peripheral nerve roots which he was able to relieve with surgery.'

They had reached Bryony's car by now and she turned to look up at him. 'So you really think it's likely that Peter might make a complete recovery?' she asked.

He sighed. 'That would be an over-optimistic prognosis. Let's just say I think it's well worth a try. You see, Peter's injuries were due to violent kickings – he wasn't crushed. And that could make all the difference.'

She shook her head doubtfully. 'He's had setbacks – if he were to be disappointed again…' She thought about the ordeal Peter had suffered in court the previous week. 'You know, of course that the man who attacked him got away with it?'

Max's eyebrows rose. 'I'd hardly say that. He'll be closely watched in future and if he puts a foot wrong he'll go down for the maximum time. Anyway, it seems it was a case of mistaken identity. He mistook Peter for someone who had robbed him.'

Bryony stared at him. 'Is that supposed to make everything all right?' she demanded hotly. 'Try telling it to Peter – I'm sure it'd cheer him up no end! That monster should have been put through the same as he gave, if you want my opinion.'

Max's eyes narrowed as he stared down at her. 'Perhaps you'd like to bring back public hangings!'

'For some crimes, yes – I almost think I *would!*' Bryony felt her heart pounding stiflingly in her breast. What did *he* know about it? How dared he trot out his glib opinions to her?

'It's a big mistake to become so involved with your patients.' He shook his head at her indignant expression. 'You've always had a vindictive streak, though, haven't you, Bryony?' he added bitterly.

She caught her breath at the accusation. 'How would *you* know how it feels to be a victim of violence?' she flung at him.

He looked steadily down at her, his dark eyes boring dangerously into hers. 'I think you underestimate my experience, Bryony. I know all about it, make no mistake,' he told her quietly. 'There are other ways to hurt than by kicking people, you know. Ways that are just as effective and damaging – just as violent in their way.' And without another word he turned and left her standing beside her car, her stomach churning with the sickeningly impotent rage she hadn't suffered for months. Injustice boiled inside her like a volcano, making her long to scream the truth across the car park after him.

Instead, she unlocked the car door and climbed in, to sit staring through the windscreen as Max's car drove past; her lower lip clamped hard between her teeth and tears trembling on her lashes.

As soon as Bryony closed the front door of the flat that evening she heard a familiar male voice in the kitchen. Graham White, the occupational psychologist, had been Alison's faithful admirer for as many years as they had worked together. They went out regularly and had occasionally shared their holidays. He usually came to dinner on the night of the monthly meetings, so Bryony wasn't surprised at his presence. She put her head round the kitchen door and greeted him before going to her room to take off her outdoor things. He was a distinguished-looking man of about forty-five, with thick silvery hair and kind blue eyes. His marriage had ended in divorce some years ago and he had been proposing to Alison regularly for the past two years.

During the meal Bryony detected a slightly uneasy atmosphere, and as soon as she had helped with the washing-up she announced that she felt like an early night and retired to her room to wash her hair and watch her portable television. She heard Graham leave at about eleven o'clock and soon after, Alison tapped on the door and came in, carrying two mugs of cocoa.

'Hi. Not asleep, then?'

Bryony shook her head. 'Of course not. I just thought you two would appreciate some time on your own.'

Alison sat on the bed and handed her one

94

of the steaming mugs. 'You must have noticed that I was a bit preoccupied,' she said. 'Graham and I came to a decision earlier this evening – one that threatens to cause a few problems.' She looked at Bryony over the rim of her mug. 'It affects you, I'm afraid.'

'Really – how come?'

'Graham asked me to marry him,' Alison said.

Bryony laughed. 'So what's unusual about that?'

'Nothing – except that this time I didn't turn him down.'

There was a pause as Bryony took in this startling piece of news, then she put down her cup and threw her arms around her aunt, hugging her hard. 'Oh, that's *great*, Alison!' she smiled. 'He's so right for you. I can't think why you didn't say yes years ago.'

'There were two very practical reasons why I didn't,' Alison told her. 'It simply wouldn't have been fair. His ex-wife was still dependent on him and his son Harry was still at school. Now it seems his wife is remarrying and his son is self-supporting at last, so there's nothing to stop us.'

'Fantastic! When's the happy day? I do

hope you're going to ask me to be a bridesmaid...' Bryony broke off, puzzled by her aunt's expression. 'What is it? You don't exactly look like an ecstatic bride-to-be.'

'I wish there was an easy way to say this, Bryony,' Alison frowned. 'Graham will be moving in here after the wedding. The lease is up on his flat and with both of us working there doesn't seem any point in buying a house...'

The truth dawned on Bryony. 'Oh – of course. You'd like me to find another flat!' She forced a laugh. 'Silly of me. As if you'd want me hanging round like a giant gooseberry!'

'There's no hurry, dear. Stay on till you find the right place,' Alison assured her. 'I don't want you to think we're turning you out.' She laid a hand on her niece's arm. 'And darling – if there's the slightest doubt in your mind about living alone, I'll...'

'Rubbish!' Bryony interrupted. 'I should have done it ages ago. I've relied on you far too long as it is. I insist that you start making plans right away. After all the years you and Graham have waited you deserve it.'

Alison hugged her. 'You're *quite* sure?' Her eyes searched Bryony's.

'Absolutely certain.'

'You know, it would do you good to mix with some young people of your own age,' Alison told her. 'I've thought for a long time now that what you need is some parties – a little fun.'

'Well, who knows – maybe you're looking at the next sensation to be launched on the social scene at the City Hospital!'

As the door closed behind Alison, Bryony allowed the bright smile to slide from her face. Switching off the bedside light, she slipped down under the covers and closed her eyes, trying hard to be happy for Alison and Graham – striving to shut out the feeling of abandonment and the terrifying prospect of being alone again. Where would she go and what would she do? a panic-stricken inner voice demanded. She took a deep breath. Everything would be all right, she told herself, trying to quell the panic. It *had* to be. This was the test she had always known would come one day, and now she must face it with all the courage she could muster.

CHAPTER FIVE

The children's ward at the City Hospital was a hive of industry. Having set the more able young patients their painting and handicraft tasks, Bryony was busy working with a small boy who had been in traction for six weeks following a severe fracture of the femur, teaching him to walk again with the aid of a walking frame and doing her best to make it seem like a game. When the gentle exercising was over and he was settled in the playroom with a jigsaw puzzle Bryony looked round for Staff Nurse Jane Fairman. She spotted her sitting at the desk in Sister's little glass-walled office, apparently catching up on some paperwork.

'I've been meaning to have a word with you,' said Bryony, looking round the door.

'Oh, good, what is it?' asked Jane, looking up. 'Anything to relieve the monotony of this! I've been putting it off for days.'

Bryony took a deep breath. 'I mustn't stop now, but – I suppose you've found a new flatmate?' she asked tentatively.

'No.' Jane put down her pen. 'Don't tell me you know of someone suitable?'

'That depends. Would you say I was suitable?' Bryony asked.

'Are you serious?' The other girl's eyes lit up. 'I can't think of anyone I'd rather share with.' She looked round, noticing that Sister was watching them from the other end of the ward. 'Look, can we meet later and have a chat about it?' She looked at her watch. 'I'm due for my lunch break at half-twelve.'

'Fine.'

'The canteen?'

'See you there. I shall be in the hospital for most of today anyway.'

When the paints had been put away and the children had had their elevenses, it was time for the games to which the children all looked forward. But while bibs were being taken off and mugs removed, Bryony went to see Nigel. The young student nurse who was with him told her that he had progressed from eggshells to paper, which he was able to tear with obvious enjoyment, smiling at the feel and sound of it. Bryony had brought him some pieces of dried fern and watched with satisfaction as he explored this new texture, the delight on his face plain to see.

'I think we'll let him sit in on the games this morning,' she told the nurse. 'Even if he can't join in it will help him to feel included.'

'Games' included music and movement and singing rhymes involving numbers and letters. The games session was designed to help the small patients with movement and co-ordination, and there was always plenty of noise and laughter as all the children joined in enthusiastically. It was a happy way to wind up the morning and as usual the time went quickly. Before Bryony knew it the ward clock had moved round to twelve o'clock.

By the time she arrived at the canteen Jane was waiting, and together they queued to collect their meal, finding a quiet table on the far side of the canteen, close to the window that overlooked the hospital grounds. As they unloaded their trays and settled themselves, Jane asked: 'So what's happened to make you spread your wings? I thought you and your aunt hit it off pretty well.'

'Oh, we do,' Bryony assured her. 'But it's time I let her have a little privacy...' She hesitated. 'Look, I'm sure she wouldn't mind me telling you – she's going to be married.

Her new husband will be moving into the flat.'

'That's great!' Jane tucked into her ham salad. 'I take it it's Graham White?'

Bryony laughed. 'Who else?'

'Well, Sheila and Derek have already moved into their house, so as far as I'm concerned you can move in whenever you're ready,' Jane told her. 'As a matter of fact I was planning a little surprise party for them. Their house is in too much of a mess to throw one there, so I thought it would be nice to have it at the flat. We could make it a sort of flatmate warming too!'

'Oh – I don't know...' The familiar feeling of not being in control of her own life began to seep back into Bryony's mind. She and Jane had always got along well together, but so far they had only mixed in the hospital environment. The other girl was so vivacious and outgoing. Had she made the right choice in offering to share with her? Since she had come to Bridgehurst she had led such a quiet, sheltered life. She had almost forgotten how to mingle happily with a crowd – how to talk to people about anything other than work.

Jane was looking at her. 'You and Geoff Mason see each other a bit, don't you? You could ask him if you like. It'll be a little reward for his helping you to move.'

'But I haven't asked him to help me.'

'No, but you're going to, aren't you? All that brawn! He's just what you need. After all, why keep a dog and bark yourself?'

Bryony laughed. 'Well, I hadn't actually thought about it, but yes – I suppose...'

'Good! That's settled, then. So when shall we say?'

Bryony felt slightly breathless, swept along on the wave of Jane's enthusiasm. Before she knew it she had arranged to move her things into Jane's flat the following Saturday – with Geoff's help – though as yet he was blissfully unaware of the fact.

They had reached the coffee stage and Jane was expounding on the subject of decorating – wallpaper versus emulsion paint, when she suddenly broke off, her attention taken by something that was happening behind Bryony at another table. 'Oh-oh, romance is definitely in the air at the City,' she said confidentially. 'First Sheila and Derek, then your aunt and Graham White. Now it seems Sara Daneman has found herself a dishy new guy. Have you seen him?'

Bryony glanced quickly over her shoulder, following Jane's gaze, but already she knew what she would see. Sara's bright head was bent close to Max's dark one over a table some six yards away as they consulted the day's canteen menu. As she watched, Max got up and crossed the room to join the food queue.

Jane's eyebrows rose as she looked at her friend. 'Now *that* has to be a sign that things are moving,' she said. 'Greater love hath no man than he will stand in the food queue for a woman!'

Sara caught them looking and waved. Getting up from the table, she walked across to them. 'Hello, you two. I met Max Anderson in the corridor and thought I'd bring him down here for lunch. Poor love's been doing post-mortems with Daddy all morning, so I think he deserves it.'

Jane pulled a face. 'I'm surprised he can fancy lunch at all, let alone the kind of food they dish up in here!' Her grimace widened as a thought occurred to her. 'Ugh! They've got liver casserole on the menu. I hope to God he doesn't choose that!'

Sara gave a scandalised little laugh. '*Jane!* You're one of the biggest ghouls I know. I shan't tell him you said that.'

'I don't care if you do! Bring him over here and I'll tell him myself,' said Jane unrepentantly. 'I've seen him about – I mean, let's face it, anyone who hadn't noticed *him* would need their eyesight testing, wouldn't they?' She wagged a finger at Sara. 'And that reminds me; I strongly resent your keeping him all to yourself, Sara Daneman – just because your daddy's a big noise at the City you think you can have first pick of all the best males in the place!'

Sara laughed, holding up her hands in mock surrender, knowing Jane's banter for what it was. 'All right – all right!' She glanced round and saw Max unloading the tray at their table. 'No time like the present. I'll call him over now.'

As she beckoned, Jane leant across to Bryony. 'Crafty so-and-so. She's only doing it now because they have hot food waiting and she'll have a good excuse to whip him away again before either of us can flutter our eyelashes at him!'

But Bryony was quite unable to join in the lighthearted badinage. It seemed that, large though the City Hospital was, she was going to run into Max with dismaying regularity. She supposed she'd better get used to it. She looked up as Sara introduced Max to Jane, her arm tucked intimately through his.

'This is Staff Nurse Jane Fairman – Jane,

105

Dr Max Anderson.' As they acknowledged each other Sara said, 'And of course you know Bryony.'

Max managed an amiable smile in her direction. 'Of course. Hello.'

'Hello.'

Jane shot Bryony a surprised look before saying: 'I've just been telling Bryony, I'm planning a party,' she said. 'My flatmate is getting married and I'm giving a little do for the happy couple. I do hope you'll both come.'

'I'm sure we'd both be delighted, wouldn't we?' Sara smiled up at Max.

He nodded briefly. 'Yes. Er – I don't want to seem rude, but our lunch...'

'Of course, don't let us keep you.' Jane waved a dismissive hand at them. 'I'll let you know when we've arranged a date, then, shall I, Sara?' She waited till the two were out of earshot, then said: 'Not exactly friendly, is he – *snob!*' She gave an indignant little snort. 'I daresay he thinks himself a little too elevated to hobnob with the likes of us!'

'I don't think they meant to be rude,' said Bryony defensively.

'Sara didn't. Sara's a love; she and I went to school together, though of course she was much brainier than me,' Jane told her. 'No, I was talking about *him*. I've met his type before. One of your strong, silent type. Hasn't been here five minutes, but you'll notice he's managed to find himself the one attractive woman doctor in the place. You won't catch *him* dating the nurses!'

'I don't think it's like that. His father was at university with Dr Daneman. They've known each other for ages.' Bryony coloured as she realised how protective she sounded – and how knowledgeable.

Jane was quick to pick this up. 'Ah yes, I meant to ask you about that.' She leaned forward, her green eyes glittering mischievously. 'How come you know so much about him already? Strikes me you're a bit of a dark horse.'

'Oh, Geoff took me out to dinner the other night and we ran into Sara and him.' Bryony could see by Jane's expression that she was about to ask another question. 'Heavens, look at the time!' she exclaimed, looking at her watch. 'I must fly. See you on Saturday, then.'

As they sat eating their last breakfast together the following Saturday morning Alison looked unhappy.

'I told you there was no hurry, Bryony,' she said for the hundredth time. 'There was no need for you to move out this quickly. Are you sure this is what you want to do?'

Bryony sighed. 'I've told you, it's a perfect arrangement. Jane has a very nice flat and she needs someone to share the rent with her. I'd never find anything half as good on my own. I didn't want to miss the chance.'

'Well, if you're really sure...' Thoughtfully, Alison poured herself another cup of coffee. 'Jane Fairman's a nice girl, of course, but she's rather extrovert. Are you sure...?'

'We understand each other,' Bryony assured her patiently. 'And anyway, who was it said I should be having more fun?'

Alison shook her head. 'You're not just doing it so as not to be on your own, are you?'

Bryony looked her aunt in the eye. 'I suppose I might be. Is there anything wrong with that? After all, I've shared with someone ever since I began my training. I'm used to it.'

'And it's not because...?'

'No! It's not *because*...' Bryony leaned across the table and patted her aunt's arm. 'For heaven's sake stop worrying about me, Alison. Think about yourself and Graham and all the plans you have to make. I'm fine, I promise you.' She looked at her watch and began to clear the table. 'Better get these things cleared away. I asked Geoff to be here by ten.'

But Alison caught her wrist. 'Wait. Sit down a minute, Bryony. There's something else I want to talk to you about, and I may not get another chance if you're really set on moving out today.'

Slowly Bryony sat down again opposite her aunt. She had a feeling that she wasn't going to like what was coming.

'It's the VES – you know, the new centre,' Alison told her. 'It opens next week. On Monday there's a special tour of inspection and an informal lecture. There'll be a woman police inspector, a counsellor and a police surgeon to talk to us.'

'*Us?*' Bryony made an involuntary move to rise from the table, but Alison put a hand on her shoulder.

'Listen. There's no getting away from it. We're all in a position to help and we could be called upon at any time, so the least we can do is to go along and find out what it's all about.'

Bryony frowned. 'I suppose you're right,' she said reluctantly. 'But surely you could fill me in on the details later?'

'I want you to *be* there, Bryony.'

When Alison looked like that Bryony knew it was useless to argue. 'All right. But I don't see why...'

'You can't push these things under the carpet for the rest of your life,' said Alison earnestly. 'Problems don't go away if you ignore them, you know. It's something that should be brought out into the open and faced. Your reaction to what Max said that evening proved that – to me if not to you. Working with...' The sound of the doorbell's shrilling brought her to a halt in mid-sentence.

Relief flooded through Bryony as she sprang to her feet. 'That'll be Geoff. I'd better let him in.'

'You will come on Monday, won't you, Bryony?' Alison called after her. 'It's at twelve o'clock – so as not to interfere with the day's appointments. Lunch will be available if...' She stopped speaking. Bryony was already in the hall, opening the door to Geoff.

Even in four years Bryony had not accumulated much in the way of belongings, and by lunchtime she had unpacked and put away most of her clothes in her new room. Geoff had been despatched to the local take-away to buy lunch for the three of them and Jane stood in the doorway of Bryony's room, a duster in her hand.

'Where are all your photographs and ornaments?' she asked, looking round. 'Sheila had hundreds. You couldn't get inside the room for china animals and framed snaps of all her sisters and brothers and their numerous infant offspring!'

'I don't have any family except Alison,' Bryony told her. 'And I doubt if she'll be presenting me with any new little cousins now.'

Jane flopped down on the bed, regarding her new flatmate thoughtfully. 'What about you and Geoff, Bry? I don't remember seeing you with anyone until you started going out with him.' She hesitated. 'Don't take this the wrong way, but I've always – well – had my doubts about him, if you know what I mean.'

'I don't know anything about Geoff's private life,' said Bryony, turning away to close the last drawer. 'We're friends, that's all. He's kind and goodnatured.'

'Oh, I know. Geoff's a lovely person, and I'm not saying anything against him. It's just...'

'I know what you mean,' Bryony said quickly. 'But it isn't an important issue – to either of us.'

Jane smiled. 'Fine. That's all right, then. Well, I'll lay the table and put the kettle on for coffee before he gets back.' She paused in the doorway. 'Bryony, I hope you can look on me as a friend,' she said quietly.

Bryony turned to look at her in surprise. 'Of course I do, Jane.'

'I mean a *real* friend.' Jane frowned and bit her lip, trying hard to find the right words. 'It's just that sometimes you have a sort of *lost* look. If there's anything bothering you I – well, I just want you to know that I can be a serious person. I know I fool around a lot, but inside I feel things as deeply as anyone – perhaps more so. So if you need a shoulder any time...'

'Thanks. I appreciate that, Jane. And I'll remember.'

The two girls smiled warmly at each other, their friendship deepening in that moment. Then the door banged shut and a voice called: 'Come and give me a hand, one of you! It's just not on, you know, leaving me to slave over a hot carrier bag all on my own!'

Geoff had gone mad in the Chinese take-away, bringing a vast selection of just about everything on the menu, from Peking duck and sweet'n'sour pork, right down to prawn fried rice and a whole galaxy of side dishes. He had even called in at the wine shop next door and lashed out on two bottles of rather dubious fizzy wine. He insisted that they ate sitting on the floor, even though Jane assured him that this was the Japanese custom.

The hour that followed proved to be quite hilarious with Geoff in his most outrageous mood, and Jane responding wittily till Bryony's stomach ached with laughter. At six o'clock John, Jane's boyfriend, arrived and the four of them went out for a drive in the country, finishing up in a tiny thatched pub for a drink. By the time Bryony fell into bed in her new room that night she felt relaxed and happy – all her doubts that she had made the right move dispelled.

Monday morning at Fenning House proved eventful. The remedial drama session went well, and Bryony found to her surprise that she had accumulated four more class members. Hearing the others so engrossed in their 'radio play', some of the others had changed their view of the drama session and turned up in the recreation room at ten o'clock, demanding to be allowed to join in.

Bryony noticed that Peter Gardner was quiet and thoughtful, however, and when the morning session came to a close she asked him to stay behind, pretending she needed his help in packing away her equipment.

When the last of the stragglers had finally gone, still arguing about who should take the role of 'James Bond', she asked him if there was anything on his mind.

'I expect you've heard,' he said, running a hand through his hair. 'They want to operate again. Something to do with these spasms I've been having.' He looked up at her unhappily. 'I know it won't help. I just wish they'd leave me alone. This means they won't let me start training for anything. If you ask me the whole thing is just a waste of time.'

'You don't have to have the new op, Peter,' Bryony told him quietly. 'The decision is yours when it comes down to it.'

'But that's just *it!*' he told her angrily. 'I don't know enough about it. I have to trust them – and if they say there's a chance I just might walk again how can I afford to pass it up? It's just that I'd got used to the idea of being like this for the rest of my life. Now I'll start hoping again, and if it doesn't work

I'll have to come to terms with it all over again.'

Bryony put her hand on his shoulder. 'Of course, I do see that.' Suddenly she saw how helpless Peter must feel; his whole future in the hands of the surgeons. Fleetingly she wondered if they possessed the imagination to put themselves in his shoes or whether he was just another challenge to them. 'Believe me, I really understand how you must feel, Peter,' she said. 'I just wish there were more I could do to help.'

He smiled up at her. 'I know. You really *do* understand, don't you? Sometimes I feel as though I'm talking to another disabled person when I talk to you. You seem to know so well what I'm feeling.'

The remark stunned Bryony. It was so obviously intended as a compliment, nevertheless she was still pondering on it later as she drove towards the hospital to keep the lunchtime appointment Alison had talked her into. Maybe Peter's chance remark was nearer to the truth than he could possibly know. Maybe in a strange way she *was* suffering from a kind of disability – though hers, unhappily, was of the kind for which there was no cure.

By the time Bryony arrived at what had been the old 'short-stay ward' the party of hospital staff invited to the lecture were already assembled. Alison was waiting for her in the reception area which was reached ideally by a side entrance of the hospital. Her face was anxious.

'Ah, there you are. I was beginning to think you'd...'

'Ducked out?' Bryony finished for her, a prickle of irritation sharpening her tone. 'I *said* I'd come, didn't I? I was held up at Fenning House. I'm afraid my patients have to come first.'

Alison chose to ignore the barb. She nodded towards the two rows of chairs that had been set out, most of which were occupied. 'Shall we sit down? I think they're about to start.' As they took their places she pointed to the three people sitting at the desk; a youngish woman in immaculate police uniform, a kindly-looking middle-aged woman and a man.

'The policewoman is Inspector Thomas,' she whispered, 'the man is Dr Mitchell, a local GP and a police surgeon, and the motherly-looking lady is an RCC counsellor.'

'I see.' Bryony was looking round her at

116

the small audience. She recognised several colleagues, social workers, senior nurses and therapists. In the back row a group of doctors sat together – among them Max. He caught her eye and nodded a brief acknowledgement. She felt the familiar sinking of her spirits, but swallowed it back determinedly as the police inspector stood up and began to speak.

In a pleasant relaxed way she told them that the new City Hospital's VES was intended first and foremost as a refuge. It would be a place where victims of all kinds of sexually related abuse could find medical treatment, counselling and above all, sanctuary. Although it would be run in conjunction with the police no one would at any time be put under pressure to report what had happened or to make a formal complaint. This would be made clear to them from the start.

'I'm sure I don't need to tell you as members of the medical profession that it is vital that victims of sexual crime receive medical care without delay,' Inspector Thomas said. 'They must have the necessary tests and preventive treatment. Also, to help them to recover from the mental trauma we hope to provide sympathetic volunteers who will just listen while they talk, or if they're unable to talk, just to sit with them.' Inspector Thomas's attractive face was serious as she stressed her point: 'I can't tell you how important this kind of work is. Believe me, there's no kinder way for anyone to give a little of their free time – even if it's only one hour a week it would be of great help, so if any of you know of suitable people perhaps you would like to get in touch with Mrs Gregson, our chief counsellor here.'

Dr Mitchell, the police surgeon, stood up next and carefully explained the medical police procedure when a case was reported; the examination necessary, the photographing of injuries and the medical and forensic tests that would supply vital evidence in the case of prosecution. As she listened, Bryony sat with her fists clenched in her lap. Her heart thudded dully in her chest and she could feel the rising tide of panic threatening to take her over. Sensing this, Alison reached out to touch her hand in silent reassurance.

After the surgeon's brief talk Mrs Gregson, the woman counsellor, took the party round the refurbished unit, showing them first a cupboard where pretty pastel-coloured tracksuits of all sizes hung.

'A victim's clothing must be tested for

forensic evidence,' she explained. 'And it's important psychologically that no woman should be obliged to wait wrapped in a blanket or some unsightly borrowed garment.'

She showed them the examination room with its restful green walls, designed to have the minimum of clinical atmosphere; the comfortably furnished rest room and, perhaps most important of all, the pretty bathrooms where the victims would be allowed to lie in warm, scented water in peace and seclusion for as long as they wanted.

Bryony walked round with the others. The panic had subsided now, but she felt oddly detached – as though only half of her were there. Her practical side knew that it was a big step forward – a marvellous idea. But the other half refused to identify with any of it. The whole situation had a dreamlike quality; she felt dissociated – unreal.

Coffee and sandwiches had been laid out when they returned to Reception, but Bryony had already decided not to stay. Making a hurried excuse to Alison, she picked up her bag and hurried out to the car park, taking great gulps of the fresh air as she emerged into the afternoon sunshine.

As she walked towards her car all the reason she had tried so hard to hang on to left her. She knew that she could on no account set foot in that place again. She acknowledged that it was a revolutionary step forward. She admired the people who had brought it into being. And she despised herself for her cowardice. But none of that made the slightest difference. This afternoon had been an ordeal and nothing, *nothing* could ever change the way she felt.

She didn't hear the hurrying footsteps behind her and when a hand descended on her shoulder and a voice spoke her name she started violently, spinning round, a shrill cry of alarm escaping her lips. She stepped backwards, almost overbalancing into one of the flower beds bordering the car park as she looked with frightened eyes at the man behind her.

CHAPTER SIX

'*Bryony!* It's all right, it's only me.' Max reached out both hands to steady her as she almost overbalanced. 'I was hoping to have a word with you about young Peter Gardner. I thought you'd be staying to eat with the rest of us.'

'I – er – no, I decided – not to...' Bryony felt the heat of her confusion and embarrassment stinging her cheeks and neck and she stood looking helplessly up at him.

He frowned slightly. 'I'm sorry. I didn't mean to startle you.'

'You didn't! I mean – I was deep in thought.'

His frown turned to a look of concern and his hands tightened on her shoulders as he said: 'It's more than that. You looked absolutely terrified when I caught you up just now. What is it, Bryony – what's the matter?'

She shook herself free of his grasp, furious at giving herself away so stupidly. 'I *told* you – I was deep in thought and you made me jump, that's all!' The protest came out as a shrill squeak and she bit her lip. She was making a complete fool of herself. To her utter horror her throat thickened and her eyes filled with tears. She struggled desperately to try and stop her lower lip from quivering.

Without another word Max took her arm and marched her the few yards to where his car was parked. Unlocking the passenger door, he opened it and pushed her firmly inside. She sat there gulping back the threatened tears, as helpless as a trapped animal as she watched him walk round the car and climb in beside her.

'Look, I'm sorry about the things I said the other day,' he said, turning to her. 'We seemed to get at cross purposes. We're not going to help the Gardner boy by carrying personal animosity into the case. It was most unprofessional.'

Bryony took a deep breath. 'I know. It was my fault too. I – said things I shouldn't too.' She felt his eyes on her and wished she could return his gaze, but she couldn't; she was still perilously close to tears. 'You wanted to talk about Peter Gardner,' she remarked, changing the subject. 'I saw him this morning, as it happens. He's desperately afraid of having further surgery; apprehensive about building his hopes up again after he'd become resigned to his condition. He's worried too about delaying his career prospects, yet he feels he can't pass up any possibility of complete recovery.' She glanced sideways at him. 'There's something else – something I don't think Peter has thought of. Even a partial recovery could affect his chances of getting compensation, and in my view he really deserves that for what he's been through.' She looked at him tentatively. 'Sometimes, Max – sometimes it's hard to put ourselves in patients' shoes – especially when we have no experience that can match what they're feeling.'

'I know. I appreciate that, Bryony – and believe me, all these things have been taken into consideration.' There was a pause, then he reached out to cup her chin, turning her face towards him. 'You *are* all right, aren't you?'

'Yes – yes, of course.'

'Surely you can't have been *that* upset by our disagreement the other day?'

'No! No, of course not. I told you...'

For a moment they looked into each other's eyes, and in that moment Bryony knew with an almost overwhelming surge of dismay that she was as much in love with him as she had ever been. Gazing into the dark eyes, now unguarded in their concern for her, she ached with regret for the unbridgeable gulf between them. His touch sparked a sharply painful memory of the warmth they had once shared – the sweet familiarity of his arms around her; she had to clench her hands into tight fists to prevent herself from reaching out to touch his face – to remind herself of the texture of his skin and the shape of the strong bones beneath it, to caress the tiny, barely visible scar on his chin. It was absurd, she told herself sternly. What was done couldn't be undone. They were both different people now – mere acquaintances. She, at least, could never go back – never again be the girl Max had once loved. With a determined effort she fought for control, carefully composing her features – was it possible that he could read her thoughts from her expression? But his eyes held hers almost hypnotically, his fingers still cradling her chin. He seemed on the brink of saying something, then changed his mind. Dropping his hand to the steering wheel, he glanced at the dashboard clock.

'Damn! I'm going to have to go.' His voice was calm and matter-of-fact, breaking the spell.

'Oh – yes. Me too.' Bryony realised that she had been holding her breath and turned away, searching feverishly for the handle of the unfamiliar car door.

He reached across to open it for her. 'Bryony, maybe we can get together again some time soon,' he said. 'To talk about Peter Gardner, I mean.'

'Oh, I don't really think there'd be any point,' she said breathlessly. 'I've no right to any say in what happens to Peter. I'm only his OT, after all.' The tension inside her was almost unbearable. His face was a hair's breadth from hers; the sweetly familiar scent of him was in her nostrils, powerfully evocative, tearing at her senses. She thrust the door open and almost fell out of the car. 'Maybe you'll be coming to Jane's party,' she said in an attempt to cover her abruptness, bending to look at him through the car window.

But his eyes had changed again. They were as hard and bright as jet as he looked back at her. 'Not if it's this week,' he said, switching on the ignition. 'I'll be tied up every evening and then I'm going home for the weekend – taking Sara to meet Dad and Aunt Lou.' His expression was cool as he looked at her. 'I expect I'll see you around, Bryony. Goodbye.'

Bryony watched him drive away with the

feeling that she had lost something, missed an opportunity. It was almost as though she had held some tremulous wild creature in her hand, only to frighten it away again with her unwitting clumsiness. She shrugged, telling herself sternly not to be so foolish. Perhaps it was simply that Max had been trying all along to put her in the picture about the relationship between himself and Sara Daneman. So he was taking her home to meet his family? Jane must have been right; there was obviously something deeper than friendship between them. As she turned away towards her own car she wondered ruefully what Aunt Lou would make of Sara. Surely she would be able to find no faults in her!

Bryony spent the first half of the afternoon in the geriatric wing of the hospital. She always felt sorry for those patients who had been admitted because of accidents in the home. There were many who had been totally independent until a fall or perhaps a fire had sent them into hospital, never to return to the happy seclusion of the homes they loved again in spite of the fact that they had made a complete recovery. Such a one was Mrs Herd, a sprightly eighty-year-old whose ancient gas cooker had exploded one morning six weeks earlier, causing her to be admitted with burns and shock. She had no relatives to care for her and after the accident it had been decided that her home was no longer habitable. She was soon to be transferred to a council home for the elderly. When Bryony arrived on Kingfisher Ward, Sister took her aside.

'Perhaps you could have a word with Annie Herd,' she said quietly. 'She seems fond of you. We've broken the news to her this morning that she won't be going home and I'm afraid she's taken it badly.' She went on to fill Bryony in on the details of the case, asking her to try to explain the situation to Annie in an acceptable way, as perhaps a daughter would have done.

Bryony found the old lady in the day room, sitting in a corner by the window. Her halo of snowy hair was as beautifully dressed as ever, but the usually erect shoulders had a defeated droop to them. Bryony went across to her.

'Hello, Annie,' she said cheerfully. 'Had you forgotten it was my day? How are you getting along with your crochet work?'

Annie shook her head. 'Haven't got the heart for it today, dear. Have they told you they're sending me to one of those places? I'm not to be allowed home. They're pulling my old place down, they tell me.'

It was so unlike Annie to be depressed. Normally the bright blue eyes and mobile mouth were always ready to laugh, but today they were dull with depression. 'I reckon this is the beginning of the end,' she said gloomily. 'Once you go into one of those places you only come out in a box, you know!'

Bryony reached out to cover one of the wrinkled hands with her own.

'Come on, Annie, this isn't like you,' she coaxed. 'It's Dunster House you're going to. I visit there regularly once a month and it has a very happy atmosphere. You'll like the company too. It must have been lonely, living alone.'

Annie gave a little grunt of scepticism. 'I've had company in here,' she said scathingly. 'Had it up to here!' She held a hand under her chin. 'There's that old girl who thinks everyone's her mum and the old man – Bert, who worked on the railway – reads his catheter chart out to you, convinced it's a railway timetable. I *ask* you...!' She gave Bryony a scandalised look, then burst spontaneously into her infectious laugh. 'Flaming madhouse in here, it is, at times!'

128

Bryony smiled. 'They can't help it, Annie,' she said gently. 'It's the way age affects some people.'

'I know that, poor old things.' The old hand tightened round Bryony's and the old woman's expression grew tense again. 'But I'm afraid *I'll* get like it too, don't you see, dear?' Annie whispered urgently. 'If I could only go home to my old house I know I'd be all right.'

'It wasn't safe any more after the explosion, Annie.' Bryony took both her hands. 'Just think – do you remember how cold it was in the winter, going out to the yard to fetch coal? And the way the pipes froze? I know it was your home and you loved it, but it must have been hard work for you. At Dunster House they have central heating. You'll never feel cold again in the winter. And all the residents there are fit, just like you. They have whist drives and outings – all kinds of things. It won't be like being in hospital at all – you'll see.'

The corners of Annie's mouth lifted and she began to look a little less depressed. 'You don't have to sell it to me, love,' she said, with a ghost of the old twinkle. 'I've got to go anyway! Ah, but it's nice to know I'll be seeing your pretty little face regularly.'

She patted Bryony's cheek affectionately and picked up the cobweb-fine crochetwork that lay in her lap. 'Well, I'd better get on with this, I suppose. It's for you, you know.'

'For me? What is it?' asked Bryony.

Annie's blue eyes twinkled. 'Why, a baby shawl, of course.' Seeing Bryony's stunned expression, she added quickly: 'Oh, all right, I know you're not married yet, but they take me a fair time to do and a pretty girl like you – you'll be tripping down the aisle in no time.' She smiled. 'Believe me, there's nothing like it for a girl – marriage and babies. I know you modern girls are all for careers, but a career can't give you a kiss and a cuddle on a cold winter's night or cheer you up when you're down.'

Bryony stood up. 'I don't think marriage is for me, Annie,' she said.

The old woman looked up at her, the bright eyes sharp and perceptive. 'Why not, girl? Something go wrong in the past, did it? You don't want to worry about that, you know. Plenty of good fish left in the sea for a lovely girl like you.'

Bryony patted Annie's shoulder. 'Well, we'll have to see, won't we? I'll see you again before you go, Annie. Goodbye. Be good now.'

Talking to Annie had curtailed the time Bryony usually spent with the other patients on Kingfisher Ward, but this was often the case in the geriatric wards. Sometimes just talking to patients with problems took priority and she had learned to be flexible about using her time there. She looked in briefly on the ward where the immobile patients were, checking the various work they were doing. Knitting and embroidery was their chief form of therapy and one old man had learned to do tapestry, the pain in his arthritic fingers almost forgotten as he pushed the needle in and out, watching the colourful pattern emerging with a new sense of pride and achievement.

Bryony and Jane had set the weekend that followed aside for decorating Bryony's bedroom at the flat. Geoff had volunteered to help and Saturday morning found the three of them in their oldest jeans and sweaters, wielding paint rollers and brushes with a will. By lunchtime they had applied the first coat of emulsion and Jane retired to the kitchen to make a snack lunch, leaving Geoff and Bryony to tidy up and survey their handiwork.

'I like the colour scheme you've chosen,'

Geoff announced, looking at the rapidly drying peach walls. 'And I hear you've been making some new pastel green curtains. Very restful.'

Bryony wiped paint from her hands. 'I love pastel shades in the bedroom,' she told him. 'Do you think we'll get it finished today?'

'Sure to,' he told her confidently. 'I'll help you hang the curtains too, if you like. If I say it myself, I made rather a good job of the ones Paul and I have in our lounge.' He grinned. 'We might even have time to go out for a meal later.'

'Oh, I think Jane has a date with John,' she said.

'I meant you and me – the two of us.' Geoff peered at her. 'That's all right, isn't it? I mean, you haven't had yourself joined to Jane by the hip or anything?'

Bryony laughed. ''Course not!'

'That's all right, then.' He grinned again. 'As a matter of fact, it better be, because I've already booked a table.'

But all through the afternoon and later, while she and Geoff were out, Bryony could not stop her thoughts from returning again and again to Max and his weekend visit home. She imagined him proudly showing off Sara to his father and aunt. They would thoroughly approve of Sara, she told herself gloomily. She had everything going for her. She was brilliantly talented as well as pretty; vivacious and bubbling over with ambition, besides being a thoroughly nice girl. No inhibitions or hang-ups about Sara. Oh yes, she was sure to be a hit with the Anderson family. And Bryony was pleased for them all, she told herself firmly. The trouble was, she couldn't make herself believe it.

Finally, after having to ask Geoff twice to repeat what he had said, she gave in; pleaded a headache and asked Geoff to take her home early. She felt mean as he saw her solicitously into the empty flat and insisted on staying to make her a hot drink, escorting her to the settee and making her put her feet up before he took himself off to the kitchen.

'You know, you put too much of yourself into your job, Bry,' he called out to her through the open kitchen door. 'Paul's just the same. I have to watch him like a hawk. He'd drive himself into the ground if I didn't stop him. You and he are very much alike, you know.'

The remark gave Bryony food for thought. Paul, Geoff's flatmate, was an accountant; a slight, willowy man with the ethereal appearance of a Victorian poet. Did she have the same wistful air about her? Was that why Geoff seemed drawn to her? Did she bring out the 'mother hen' in him?

Geoff brought the steaming mug of malted milk to her as she lay on the settee, feeling a complete fraud. She made to get up, but he pressed her back against the cushions he had carefully arranged, seating himself on a stool beside her.

'Do as you're told. Drink this and try to relax. You've been on edge all evening.' He smiled ruefully at her. 'Did you think I couldn't tell?'

Obediently, she drank the hot milky drink, smiling back at him. 'You're too good to me, Geoff. If I was as preoccupied as that it can't have been very flattering. I should have realised how rude I was being.'

He took the empty mug from her and put it on the table. 'Surely we've got past the stage in our relationship where we have to be on our best behaviour all the time.' He touched her shoulder. 'I like looking after people, Bryony, especially you. One day I'd like to have a family of my own – if the right girl will have me, that is. And I think by now you must have a pretty good idea who I'd like that girl to be.' His expression was tender and wistful as he bent towards her, kissing her gently on the lips; sliding the arm that rested on her shoulder around her, to draw her close.

With her panic-stricken heart thudding sickeningly in her ears, Bryony thrust him from her and leapt to her feet. 'Geoff! Look, I'm sorry, but I can't – I had no idea, you see – I thought you were...' Despair and regret washed over her as she saw Geoff's expression change from hurt to shocked disbelief as he realised what she was trying to say.

'My God! You thought I was... You took it for granted that because Paul and I...'

'*Don't!*' She covered his mouth with her hand. 'Please, Geoff, don't say it. I'm so ashamed, please believe me.' Without realising it she had moved defensively to the back of the settee, putting it between herself and Geoff. He stood up and reached out his hand to her.

'Come and sit down, Bryony,' he said calmly. 'I think we should talk, don't you?'

Bryony's eyes filled with tears as she looked at him. Of all the people in the world Geoff was the last one she wanted to hurt. He led her back round the settee, then, sensing the fear in her, he went to sit in the chair opposite. 'First, let me tell you about

Paul,' he said quietly. 'We were at school together. He was a clever boy, but quiet and shy, and as a result of both these things he got bullied a fair bit. Then his parents split up and neither of them seemed to want him very much. After that everything started getting to him badly.' Geoff shrugged. 'I was always respected – for my size and my performance on the football field more than anything else.' He smiled ruefully. 'You know what schoolboys are like. I just sort of assumed the position of Paul's "minder" and we've been close friends ever since. He's still a bit helpless, and I suppose old habits die hard.' Bryony opened her mouth to say something, but he held up his hand. 'You're not the first to make that mistake, Bryony,' he told her. 'And I can't blame you, thinking about it. Unfortunately we live in an age where you can't have a close friendship with someone of the same sex without it being assumed that there's more to it.'

'I wasn't judging you,' Bryony told him quickly. 'I don't have any rigid opinions or prejudices. It was just that I – just...'

'That you felt *safe* with me?' he supplied, looking at her enquiringly. She nodded unhappily and he went on: 'Well, for what it's worth, that's my story.' He paused. 'So what's yours, Bryony? What happened to you? I know you broke off your engagement to Dr Anderson and I wouldn't dream of pressing you to tell me why. But it's clear to me that you had a traumatic experience at some time or other; something that seriously warped your opinion of men.' He shook his head. 'I'm still not pressing – but if you want to tell me…' His eyes searched hers. 'I honestly think you should tell someone, love – for your own good.'

Bryony looked down at the hands that lay twisted in her lap, fighting the rising tide of tears. 'I'm so bad at – at *life*,' she said helplessly. 'I don't seem to be able to relate to people properly. I'm always saying and doing the wrong thing – hurting those I don't want to hurt.'

Geoff edged his chair closer, though he carefully restrained his natural impulse to touch her. 'That's just not true, Bry,' he told her. 'You're good at your job – damned good – and that's all to do with people.' He shook his head. 'There's more to it than that, though, honey, isn't there?'

She looked up at him, meeting the clear blue eyes, then, very slowly and painfully, bit by bit, she told him what had happened to her that morning four years ago – and the shattering effect it had had on her life. Once she had started she found herself unable to stop; she heard the words come pouring out of her, releasing the tension tightly coiled within her, spilling out the poison of mistrust, suspicion and hate – the canker of guilt and self-denigration.

'And you never reported it?' Geoff said quietly when at last she paused for breath.

She shook her head. 'Alison took me to another town, to a woman doctor friend of hers, for the necessary – tests.' She shuddered at the memory. 'That was bad enough. Facing the rest – the ordeal of going to the police, of standing up in court – facing the man...' She shook her head. 'I couldn't do it – then or now. But you see that makes me feel guilty too.' She looked into his eyes. 'I'm a mess, Geoff; a mass of complexes and inhibitions, terrified of being alone – afraid of men – afraid to trust, sometimes I feel I don't really know who or what I am any more. And when *Max* turned up – here in Bridgehurst...'

'I can imagine. It reawakened the whole thing, like opening an old wound.' Very slowly Geoff moved across to sit beside her. 'Bry, let me ask you something. Now that you know I'm not – as you thought, how do you feel about me?' As she raised her face to look at him, he added: 'The *truth* please. I'm not going to be hurt if you say you can't trust me either. I'm not a fool.'

She shook her head. 'Oh, Geoff, of course I trust you. Nothing's changed – except that...' She paused, biting her lip.

Geoff spoke the thought that was in her mind: 'Except that you're still in love with Max Anderson – is that it?'

She nodded. 'That's why I've been such poor company. You see, I know that nothing could ever be the same for us. What happened changed us both. Max is different too – and anyway, he's in love with Sara Daneman now. He's taken her home this weekend to meet his family.' She shook her head impatiently. 'Oh, I'm not sure it would ever have worked between us.' She looked at him. 'I'll just have to make myself come to terms with it – all over again.'

'And all this time he thinks you jilted him?' Geoff shook his head. 'Why don't you tell him?'

She stared at him. 'I couldn't possibly!'

'You told *me*.'

'It's different,' she told him. 'You see, when Max and I were engaged I always had such high ideals – naïve, I suppose, in this day and age. I'm not the way he saw me any more. I felt – *feel* like an impostor, a fraud. I'm just not sure of myself any more.'

He frowned. 'That's ridiculous! You're sure you still love him. Maybe he feels the same, and if he does... Look, *I'm* not what you thought me, yet you say that makes no difference.'

Bryony shook her head miserably. 'Oh, Geoff, that's something different. Max will never forgive me for what I did – and anyway, I told you; for him there's someone else now.'

Gently he reached out and took her hand. 'Poor Bryony! I wish I could help, but I can't. It's up to you, love – your decision.' He looked down at her hand. 'There is one thing, though. I don't know if you realise it, but you've taken a big step forward this evening,' he told her. 'You've talked about your ordeal to me – a member of the opposite sex. *You've trusted a man.*' He grinned his dear familiar grin at her. 'I reckon that has to go down as some kind of breakthrough, don't you?'

She returned the pressure of his warm hand gratefully, nodding tremulously. 'Perhaps it does, Geoff,' she whispered. 'Perhaps you're right. I hope so.'

CHAPTER SEVEN

After her successful experiment with the residents at Fenning House Bryony was encouraged to try remedial drama with a group of physically handicapped children who regularly attended the welfare clinic's day centre. She found them far less inhibited than the group at Fenning House, eager and willing to start 'pretending' without any coaxing.

She started by discussing with them what theme they should choose, showing them the box of make-up, wigs and masks she had brought with her, borrowed from the wardrobe of the City Hospital's amateur dramatic group. As the children explored the box with its sticks of greasepaint, the strange wigs and masks, their imagination was soon stimulated. After some noisy argument they finally agreed to choose as their theme, 'sailing to a South Sea island'. The first half hour of their session was happily occupied in dressing up and trans-forming themselves. With Bryony's help

141

each chose the role he or she would play. Tactfully, she suggested that the children in wheelchairs played the 'explorers', using their chairs first as a boat and then as horses. The more mobile children dressed up in the masks and wigs and became instant 'cannibals', some of them ending by looking quite fearsome.

When the time came for them to act their story they had none of the inhibitions of the Fenning House group as they sailed their boat, sighted land and came ashore to fight a fierce battle with the island's cannibals, complete with bloodcurdling yells. But finally they all became friends, and when the staff brought in the mid-morning milk and biscuits, it immediately became a campfire meal, shared by explorers and the now tamed and friendly cannibals. The memory of the children's enjoyment lifted Bryony's spirits as she made her way back to the flat for lunch.

Jane was enjoying a brief break before being transferred to the Accident and Emergency Department and had promised to cook lunch for them both. 'It'll be better than sandwiches or the canteen, and we can catch up with the weekend gossip,' she'd said as they parted company that morning.

And although Bryony had agreed she knew she would not be confiding to Jane what had passed between herself and Geoff the night before.

Lunch consisted of a delicious steak, grilled to perfection and accompanied by a crisp salad. Bryony complimented her friend as she leaned back in her chair and prepared to enjoy a cup of coffee.

'Oh, I enjoy cooking when I've got the time,' Jane told her. 'But guess who I met when I was out shopping.'

'I feel far too lazy to try,' laughed Bryony. 'You're going to have to tell me.'

'Sara. We had a coffee together,' Jane told her. 'She's having a couple of days off too, so we were able to have a lovely long girlish gossip.'

Bryony felt herself stiffen, the delicious replete feeling which had left her feeling so relaxed vanished as she braced herself for what was to come.

'She went away with Max Anderson for the weekend!' Jane giggled. 'To stay with his father and aunt, would you believe? I asked her if she was getting the once-over as a prospective wife for the delectable Max.'

'Oh? And what did she say?' asked Bryony, her mouth dry.

'Her reply was quite unrepeatable!' Jane laughed. 'You'd be surprised what a bad influence those registrars can be. She never used language like that till she started hobnobbing in the surgeons' common room. *Common's* the operative word there, if you ask me!'

Bryony tried hard to make herself join in Jane's laughter. 'So you don't think there's anything serious going on there after all?' she asked, trying to sound casual. But Jane wagged a finger.

'Ah, I wouldn't say *that* exactly. I got the feeling she was just being evasive. She did part with one interesting piece of news, though. It seems she got quite friendly with this Aunt Louise character. The old lady took quite a shine to our Sara, so it seems, and she let her into a few family secrets. It appears that a year or two ago Max was engaged to a nurse at the hospital where he trained. Well, it seems she jilted him – left him flat!' Jane spread her hands in disbelief. 'Not easy to believe, is it? The girl must have been out of her tiny mind, if you ask me. She just took off one day about a fortnight before the wedding, leaving the poor guy a note saying: "Thanks, but no thanks!" Apparently it hit him like a ton of bricks at the time.' She shook her head. 'Imagine how he must have felt, having to face all his friends – send all the presents back! Apparently all the invitations had been sent out – *everything!* You know what hospitals are like, the gossip must have been horrendous. The wretched girl couldn't have loved him at all to let him in for that kind of punishment. She must have been completely heartless!' Jane cut herself a large slice of cheese and began to butter a biscuit. 'Anyway, it seems he swore never to have anything to do with women again, and Sara's the first girl he's taken home since.' She winked. 'That's why I say Sara was being evasive. After all, she wouldn't want to scare him off by allowing a lot of rumours to spread, would she?' She drained her cup. 'I must say I see him in quite a different light now. Now that I know what happened to him it explains that stand-offish attitude of his. It just shows – you can never tell, just looking at people, what they've been through, can you?' Pouring herself and Bryony another cup of coffee, she asked conversationally: 'Well, what did you do? Did you and Geoff have a nice evening?'

Bryony drank her coffee quickly and got up from the table on legs that felt distinctly shaky. 'Yes, very nice, thanks,' she said, gathering her things together for her afternoon calls. 'No time to tell you about it now, though. If I don't move I'm going to be late.' At the door she paused, looking back at her friend. 'Oh, by the way – about Geoff. We were wrong about him. Just thought I should tell you.'

For a moment Jane looked startled, then a smile spread over her face. 'Well, *well*,' she said. 'What d'you know?'

As Bryony pulled on her coat Jane looked up. 'Oh, that reminds me – I thought we'd have the party this Saturday. Is that all right with you and Geoff?'

The last thing Bryony felt like at that particular moment was planning a party, but she managed to smile. 'Yes, I think so. I'm not sure about Geoff, though. I'll have to ask.'

'Good. Sara said she's free and she was pretty sure that Max would be too. He's away for a few days, doing a course on ballistics at the moment.' Jane pulled a face. 'Some grisly subjects these fuzz medics have to study, don't they?'

All the enjoyment Bryony had derived from her lunch was forgotten as she went downstairs to her car and tried to prepare her mind for the afternoon's work. So Aunt Lou had been filling Sara in about Max's past, had she? She wondered briefly whether Max had told his father about running into her again here at Bridgehurst City Hospital, but dismissed the thought. Surely he wouldn't be anxious to reopen that particular subject, especially on the occasion of Sara's first visit.

As she negotiated the busy traffic in the city centre she wondered what Aunt Lou's reaction would be if she knew that Sara and she knew each other, or Sara's, were she to find out that Max's runaway fiancée was none other than Bryony Slade, whom she saw almost daily. The situation was ludicrous. It would almost be laughable – if it wasn't hurting so much!

At least with Max away Bryony was able to relax over the days that followed, secure in the knowledge that she wasn't likely to run into him around the hospital. Thinking about it, she felt fairly sure that he wouldn't be at Jane's party either, knowing that *she* would be there. He had made that abundantly clear on their parting the other day.

It was Thursday afternoon before she ran into Geoff in the City Hospital car park.

When she invited him to the party he accepted, looking pleased.

'I thought I might not hear from you again,' he confessed, falling into step beside her.

Bryony looked up at him in surprise. 'Not hear from me? Why should you think that?'

He shrugged. 'When one confides in a person one sometimes regrets it. Besides,' he smiled ruefully at her, 'there were other reasons.'

She tucked her hand into the crook of his arm. 'Good friends aren't that easy to come by, Geoff,' she told him. 'You were very kind to me the other night. I'd like to think I might have the chance to return the compliment some day.'

They were walking along the secluded path at the back of the Admin Block when he stopped walking suddenly and drew her round to face him. 'Bry, you know I'd never betray your confidence, don't you?'

'Of course, Geoff,' she told him gravely. 'That's one thing I'm a hundred per cent sure of.'

'But if I were to offer you some advice, would you take it?'

She smiled. 'I might take it, Geoff, but acting on it, though – that's something I can't promise.'

He laughed. 'That's what I thought you'd say. Still, I can always try, can't I?'

'You're going to press me to talk to Max again, aren't you?' she said. 'If you are, you might as well forget it. I have it on very good authority that he and Sara Daneman are – well, close.'

'Nevertheless, I still think you should tell him the truth about why you ran out on him,' Geoff persisted. 'Do you really want him to go on thinking the worst of you?'

'It doesn't matter now what he thinks of me, Geoff,' Bryony said firmly. 'It's over and done with. No one can ever wipe it out. Max is obviously happy now and I'm sure he wouldn't thank anyone, least of all me, for raking over old ashes.'

Geoff slapped his forehead with the palm of his hand and gave a little growl of exasperation. 'There are times, Bry Slade, when I could cheerfully try *knocking* some sense into you! – if I didn't love you dearly I *would!*' He gave her a little shake by way of illustration, then bent his head to drop a kiss on the top of her head. Feeling her stiffen and noticing that she was staring past him, he turned to see Max Anderson striding towards them along the path. 'Ah, hello,

149

Max,' he said cheerfully, his arm still round Bryony's shoulders. 'Someone said you'd been on a ballistics course. That must have been interesting. I'd like to hear all about it some time.'

Max nodded curtly. 'Afternoon, Geoff – Bryony. Can't stop now, I'm afraid I have an appointment.' His dark eyes were expressionless as he walked past them briskly and went into the building.

Geoff looked at Bryony and found her pale and trembling. He shook his head. 'He still really gets to you, doesn't he?' he said gently. 'You might keep on insisting that it's over and done with, but I'm afraid you don't convince me. The point is – can you convince yourself?'

Bryony hadn't seen Alison since she moved in with Jane. There were still a few of her things left at the flat, and she decided to call in and pick them up on her way home that evening. She found Alison in the kitchen, wearing her striped apron and preparing a meal which was quite obviously intended for more than one.

'Ah, you're busy,' she said, putting her head round the door. 'I won't stop. I just wanted to collect my...'

'Wait!' Alison strode after her through to the living room. 'You've been avoiding me, haven't you – ever since the meeting at the new crisis centre? You must have known I'd be anxious to hear your reactions.'

Bryony turned to face her. 'I haven't been avoiding you, Alison. I've been busy, that's all.'

'Well, now that you're here you can jolly well sit down for ten minutes and have a glass of sherry with me,' her aunt said firmly. 'Graham and I have set the date for the wedding. It's less than a month away, so you and I have some talking to do.'

'But surely we can meet some other time for that,' protested Bryony. 'Your guests – and the meal – won't it spoil?'

'No, it won't!' Alison went to the small table in the corner and poured two glasses of dry sherry. Handing one to her niece, she sat down in the chair opposite. 'My *guest* is only Graham, and he might as well get used to unpunctual meals if he's marrying me. As for the meal, it's a casserole, and now it's in the oven it will cook itself.' She took a sip from her brimming glass and looked up expectantly. 'First, what did you think of the VES? It's a great step forward, don't you think?'

Bryony gulped down a mouthful of sherry,

spluttering slightly over it as she replied: 'I – suppose it is. Yes, of course.' She looked pleadingly at her aunt. 'Oh, Alison, surely you don't need me to tell you? I couldn't get out of the place fast enough, if you really want to know.'

The other woman sighed. 'That's a pity.' She paused, fingering the stem of her glass. 'A case came in just yesterday; a girl of seventeen. She was quite badly injured – bad enough to need twenty-four hours in intensive care. She's OK now – at least, physically she's on the mend.' Alison leaned forward. 'This case really should be reported, Bryony,' she said urgently. 'The man must be a maniac, and if he isn't caught he'll do it again. Look, I know how you feel, but will you talk to her?'

Bryony felt cornered. 'I'd – I'd like to help, Alison – honestly I would,' she stammered. 'But I just don't see what I could do.'

'You didn't report, and you know how you felt, and *still* feel about it,' Alison pressed. 'Anyway, it would help her to talk to someone who knows from experience how she's suffering.'

'I couldn't press anyone to report,' Bryony said quietly. 'After hearing about the pro-cedure the other day – knowing what the poor girl would have to go through on top of what I know she's already suffered – I couldn't ask *anyone* to go through that.'

'But coping with the responsibility – with the knowledge that it might happen to someone else – maybe a child...?'

Bryony shook her head. 'If she did report it, and the man *was* caught, the chances are that the case would be dismissed,' she said. 'You know the legal side of it as well as I do. The victim can't prosecute – only the police can do that – and if there's the slightest doubt in their minds...' She shook her head. 'If you could only imagine what it feels like not to be believed, Alison, you'd understand. To summon up enough courage to tell a sceptical stranger about this horror you've been through, only to be cross-examined as though you're making the whole thing up!'

'The police we're working with are kind and sensitive. They must ask questions. They *have* to be sure, Bryony,' urged Alison. 'You must see that.'

Bryony put her glass down on the coffee table. 'No victim should be pressured to do it. I won't be a party to it. No one has the *right* to expect that of anyone. When all is said and done the victim is a victim all the way through. She should decide for herself.'

She stood up. 'I'm sorry, Alison.'

'Just *talk* to her, then?' Alison begged. 'Just to help her through it – for *her* sake.'

At the door Bryony paused, her shoulders drooping. 'I can't.' She spun round angrily. 'What are you trying to do to me, Alison? You already know how guilty I feel. Do you want to pile even more guilt on to my shoulders – is that it? *Why can't you leave me alone?*' Ignoring her aunt's pleas to come back and talk – calm down, she ran out of the flat and down the stairs. Sitting in the car, waiting for her hands to stop trembling, she thought for the first time of the unknown girl, lying in a bed somewhere in that vast impersonal hospital. Had she any relatives to turn to – could she talk to them if she had? Was she suffering the same mixture of nightmare emotions that Bryony remembered all too well? A sick feeling churned her stomach and her eyes filled with tears of compassion. Why *couldn't* she help? she asked herself angrily. Why did the mere thought of it fill her with stark, blind panic? If she'd felt guilty before, she positively despised herself now.

When Bryony woke on Saturday morning her first thought was that this was the day of the party. Her heart sank and she turned over in bed, hiding her face in the pillow. Sara and Max would be there. All evening she would have to force herself to smile at them – to appear relaxed and happy. Thank God Geoff would be around to help her!

All day long she and Jane busied themselves preparing for the evening; shopping in the morning, preparing food all afternoon. It was about half-past five when the telephone rang. Jane was in the bath, so Bryony answered it.

'Hello, Bryony Slade here.'

'Bryony, it's me, Sara. Look, love, I'm sorry, but I shan't be able to come to the party this evening.'

'Oh, why not?' asked Bryony.

'I've had to swap duties with a colleague who's not well,' Sara explained. 'There's a sort of summer 'flu bug going round and he's gone down with it. I couldn't say no.'

'Oh well, it can't be helped. I'm sure Jane will understand,' Bryony assured her. 'We'll have to get together another time.'

'Goodbye, then. Have a good time.'

As Bryony replaced the receiver she heaved a sigh of relief. Now she could relax and enjoy the party. She wouldn't have to spend the evening avoiding Max's eyes after all.

Later, as Bryony was dressing for the party, Jane came into her room. She eyed her friend shrewdly, watching as she zipped up the beige dress and flicked a comb through her short hair. Finally she could bear it no longer and asked: 'Why don't you wear something brighter, Bryony? After all, it *is* a party.'

Bryony looked round in surprise. 'Because I haven't got anything brighter, I suppose.' She turned to look at herself in the mirror. 'Why, does this look terrible?'

'No-o,' Jane looked at her friend critically through the mirror, her head on one side. 'It's just...' She threw herself down on the bed and turned to face Bryony. 'Oh, look – I've got to say it. You don't seem to have the first idea how to bring out the best in yourself, Bry!' She held her breath. 'There, now I suppose you'll never speak to me again!'

Bryony couldn't help laughing at the other girl's comic expression. 'Don't be silly. I know my clothes are boring. I'm afraid I don't take much interest in the way I look.'

'Well, you should. You're very attractive, you know. You have a lovely complexion and the most gorgeous eyes. It's such a waste to go around hiding your light under a bushel, as they say.' Jane went out of the room abruptly, to reappear a moment later carrying a dress over her arm. It was made of a soft, shimmering silk in a vibrant flame red. She held it against Bryony. 'You'd look fantastic in this,' she said. 'We're about the same size. Try it on.'

Bryony shook her head. 'I couldn't! Your dress?'

'Don't worry, no one has ever seen me in it,' Jane assured her. 'It was one of those impulse buys and a big mistake. With my colouring I look like some sort of femme fatale – but with your dark hair and eyes and that pale ivory skin, you'll look stunning!'

Bryony looked doubtful. 'Oh, I don't know – I've never worn red.'

'Then it's high time you did! I'm sure it's your colour. Go on, try it,' coaxed Jane. 'I've got an idea for your hair too. While you're getting into the dress I'll just get my hot-brush – and I'm sure I've got a lipstick just the right shade too.'

Fifteen minutes later Bryony stood before the dressing table mirror, staring dazedly at a reflection she hardly recognised. The dress was a more subtle colour than she had first thought – a sort of sunset colour, like the dahlias her father used to grow. It fitted her as though it had been made for her. The bodice was sleeveless, held up by the thinnest of straps, the warm colour bringing out the creamy tones of her skin. The waistline was smooth and the skirt fell in soft folds, ending in a soft, full hemline that swirled about her legs as she walked. With her hot-brush, Jane had skilfully lifted the closely cut hair so that it framed Bryony's face in attractive elfin curls. Now she stood back to admire her work, her eyes sparkling with delight.

'Well, what do you think?'

Bryony didn't know what to say. It was so long since she had looked like this – so long since she had felt a frisson of excitement looking at her own reflection. 'I don't know,' she said hesitantly. 'Isn't it a bit – a bit – er...'

'No, it *isn't* a bit – er...' laughed Jane. 'You look the way you *should* look for once in your life!' She glanced at her watch. 'Anyway, you haven't got time to change now, even if you want to. The first of the...' Her sentence was interrupted by a sharp ring at the door bell which made Bryony jump violently. Jane threw down her brush and leapt up. 'There, what did I tell you? They're here. You're on, girl. Good luck!'

Much to Bryony's relief it was Geoff's voice she heard as she stood with her ear to the bedroom door as Jane went to answer the door. She took his hand and led him inside, pouring him a drink and then holding up a conspiratorial finger.

'Wait there.' She went out of the room, to return a second or two later standing back in the doorway to reveal the transformed Bryony. 'Ta-raaa!'

Geoff stopped, his glass halfway to his lips, staring at her.

Jane laughed. 'Geoff, I hate to tell you, but your mouth's hanging open.'

He gulped hard. 'Bryony? he said, standing up and taking a step towards her. 'What have you done? You look – well, *beautiful* is the only word I can think of.'

'Oh, charming! That carries the suggestion that it's unusual for her to look beautiful,' laughed Jane mischievously.

Geoff took Bryony's hands. 'Bry knows what I mean, don't you, Bry?'

She laughed, her eyes shining. 'Do I really look all right, Geoff? You're sure it's not over the top?'

'You look a bit better than "all right",' he assured her. 'A *lot* better, in fact.'

Guests began to arrive thick and fast after

that, including Jane's ex flatmate Sheila and her fiancé. After the first tense half-hour Bryony began to enjoy herself. The only stares she received were frankly admiring. No one seemed to think she looked odd, and several of her female colleagues made a point of admiring her dress and asking her where she'd had her hair done.

At ten o'clock Jane announced that supper was served and opened the doors that concealed the small dining recess where they had laid out the buffet. Everyone was happily helping themselves to food when there was a sudden ring at the bell. Jane, in the middle of slicing ham, looked at Bryony.

'Be a love and get that, will you?'

'Of course.'

Bryony went into the tiny hallway, closing the door carefully on the packed room. Had they been making too much noise? Was it one of their neighbours, come to complain? Words of apology on her lips, she opened the door – then stood staring with shock at the man outside.

'Max! I – we weren't expecting you,' she stammered. 'Sara rang to say...'

'I know. I'm sorry. Would you like me to go away again?'

'Oh, no! It's just that I wasn't...' She

swallowed the rest of the sentence and held the door open. 'Please come in.'

He stepped inside. 'I know I'm terribly late, but I thought that one of us should put in an appearance.' He handed her a wrapped bottle. 'Oh, look, you'd better have this.'

'Thanks. Er – can I take your coat?'

He looked down at her as they stood crowded together in the narrow hallway. 'Actually, I'm not wearing one.'

She blushed, feeling foolish. 'Oh, no. Well – er – do come through. We've only just started supper.'

Jane tried hard to keep her eyebrows under control when she saw Bryony leading Max into the room. She took Bryony's arm and drew her to one side.

'Look, I don't think Max knows very many of the people here,' she whispered. 'See he gets something to eat and drink; introduce him round a bit – you know the kind of thing.' She unwrapped the bottle he had brought. 'I'll just open this and put it with the rest.' She disappeared into the kitchen.

Bryony felt trapped. She didn't want Max to think she was leaving him high and dry – yet she didn't want him to think she was hanging round him either. After all, he was quite old enough to take care of himself, she told herself. Hoping for help, she looked around for Geoff, but he was deep in conversation with one of his physio colleagues, a tall, athletic girl called Alexis. She couldn't expect help from that quarter.

At the buffet table she made sure that Max had something to eat and drink, then she prepared to melt gracefully into the background. But Max looked enquiringly at her.

'There are a couple of vacant chairs over in that corner. Will you join me?'

She nodded helplessly.

'I'm not keeping you from your other guests, am I?'

'Not at all.' She followed him to the two chairs against the wall.

'Peter Gardner is having his op next Wednesday,' he told her, when they were seated. 'Jon Keller has agreed to come over from St Hildred's to do it himself and he's asked me to assist.'

Bryony began to toy unenthusiastically with the food on her plate. 'Oh? Isn't that going to cause resentment at the City?'

'Oh, no,' he assured her. 'After all, everyone knows that Kellet is an expert in this field, and I've worked with him. It's more convenient for him to have someone who's familiar with his methods.'

'I see. And it was your idea, of course, so I suppose you deserve to be in on it.' Bryony was quiet, busy with thoughts of her own. Peter had been away at the hospital having tests when she had visited Fenning House this week. She must make a point of seeing him on Monday, to wish him luck.

'You still haven't much of an opinion of surgeons, have you?' Max asked quietly. 'You still think of them as self-centred.'

'No. I just feel specially sorry for Peter,' she told him. 'He has no relatives – no one to advise him, to be on his side.' She almost added: *And I know how that feels.* Instead, she made herself smile. 'I hope you had a nice weekend at home,' she said, deliberately changing the subject.

'Very nice,' he said. 'Dad and Aunt Lou hadn't seen Sara since she was about ten.'

'Really? They must have seen a great change in her,' said Bryony. 'I'm sure they approved.'

Max nodded. 'I think so.' Someone put on a particularly loud record and those who had finished eating got up to dance. Max looked at her. 'I'd like to talk to you, Bryony,' he said above the noise. 'This doesn't seem to be the ideal place for it, though.'

Her heart turned a somersault. *Talk? What did he mean – talk?* 'No, I don't suppose it is,' she agreed.

There was a pause, then he asked: 'Would it ruin things here if you slipped away for half an hour?'

Bryony took a deep breath to try to control the hammering inside her chest. She was being utterly ridiculous. Obviously he wanted to talk to her about Peter. He knew she felt deeply on the subject of treating patients impersonally and he was anxious to defend himself and his profession. 'I don't think so,' she said lightly. 'After all, supper's over now and we weren't going to wash up until...'

'I daresay there's still time to catch a drink somewhere,' he interrupted, looking at his watch. 'I know a quiet little wine bar.' He glanced across at Geoff, who was now dancing with Alexis. 'Is *he* going to mind if I take you away from the party? I mean, are you here together?'

'Not really. Of course he wouldn't mind.' She put down her plate. 'I'll go and tell him – and Jane.'

'I don't want to make things difficult for you...'

'No, you won't.'

Jane looked mystified until Bryony told her that Max wanted to discuss Peter Gardner's case.

'Can't you take *one* evening out to enjoy yourself?' she asked. Then, seeing Bryony's apologetic expression, she added: 'Oh, go on then – workaholic! I give up on you, I really do.'

Geoff's reaction was quite different. 'Fine – off you go,' he said happily. Turning to catch at her hand as she turned away, he whispered: 'Good luck, love. And remember my advice. You only have to say it once!'

Closing the door on the music and chatter of the party, they walked down the stairs and out into the night together. It was a warm mellow evening, with a scattering of stars and a bright new moon piercing a velvet sky.

'My car's over there,' Max pointed. 'The place I told you about is on the other side of the city. Shall we go?'

CHAPTER EIGHT

The wine bar Max had mentioned was in the older part of the city, in what had been the cellar of one of the city's oldest inns. It was full of atmosphere somewhat spoilt by the inevitable piped music. They found the place almost deserted, but the friendly barman explained that it was too late for the early diners and too early for the post-theatre crowd. He gave them a menu to study over their drinks, but Bryony said she wasn't hungry.

'You didn't touch your supper back at the party,' Max observed. 'I suspect that might have been my fault. Do have something.'

The barman helpfully suggested a seafood salad, the chef's speciality, and finally she agreed – mainly because she could feel the man's shrewd eye on her and didn't want to invite his speculation.

Max chose a table on the far side of the room. The natural arch of the cellar formed a secluded booth under which a table was flanked by two buttoned leather banquettes.

The barman brought their food across, asking them if there was any particular music they'd like. 'Might as well have what you want, seeing you've got the place to yourselves, eh?' He winked at Max and Bryony felt her colour rising. Clearly he thought they were out for a romantic evening together and was doing his best to help the mood along.

When he had withdrawn to stand quietly polishing glasses behind the bar, Max smiled at her. 'Do try to relax, Bryony. I'm not going to eat you.'

She picked up her knife and fork and began to attack her salad. 'I'm perfectly relaxed, thank you,' she told him. Max had certainly changed, she realised it even more now. It wasn't just his appearance, the leaner face and the touch of silver in his hair. There was an air of quiet authority about him, a commanding presence that made her uneasy. She knew instinctively that he was a man who would not be fobbed off; once he made his mind up to get at the truth it would be hard to deter him. She wished unhappily that she had stayed at the party, in the comparative safety of the crowded flat. 'W-What was it you wanted to talk to me about?' she asked diffidently. 'I take it it has something to do with Peter Gardner's operation.'

'No, it hasn't.' Max sighed. 'Look, Bryony, believe me, this isn't easy for me. I didn't want to come to that party this evening and when Sara had to cancel I was relieved.' He leaned forward. 'I didn't want to come. But then I found I couldn't stay away. Can you understand that?' His eyes burned relentlessly into hers till she quietly laid down her knife and fork, giving up all pretence of enjoying her food.

'I – think so.'

'I argued with myself that it was all over and done with,' he went on, 'that I didn't give a damn any more. Once I'd got over the first shock of seeing you again I told myself that it didn't matter – that I could live with it. But I can't; at least, not like this. There are so many loose ends, Bryony; so many things I have to know.'

There was a pause as his eyes held hers. She wondered if he could possibly imagine how desperate she felt at that moment – viewing the prospect of the lies she was going to have to fabricate in order to supply the answers to the unspoken questions in his voice and his eyes.

He leaned forward. 'Why, Bryony?' he

asked her simply. 'What on earth made you run away like that?' He frowned. 'Why Bridgehurst – and why change to occupational therapy when you were so close to qualifying?'

She took a deep breath. 'The reason for coming to Bridgehurst is easy. Alison, my aunt, lives and works here, as you might possibly remember.' Her fingers were twisted together in an agonised white-knuckled grip out of sight under the tablecloth. 'I – just wanted to make a completely fresh start. I suddenly felt that nursing wasn't for me, and Alison suggested OT. There was a shortage of therapists here. Studying helped to take my mind off...' She trailed off.

'Off what?' Max's voice had lost its softness. 'Off *me?* You suddenly felt that *I* wasn't for you either; is that what you're saying? Was I such a – such a monster?'

She shook her head frantically. 'No, Max – *no!*' It was impossible to think of a reasonable excuse. Out of the corner of her eye she caught the barman's vigilant eye. At the sound of her protesting voice he had stopped polishing the glass he was holding and was looking across at them with curiosity. 'Please,' she whispered. 'We're attracting attention.'

Max swore softly under his breath. Turning, he held up a hand to the man. 'Can we have two brandies, please?'

Suddenly galvanised into action, the barman sprang to attention. 'Right, sir. Two brandies coming up!'

'I don't want a brandy,' Bryony protested.

'Yes, you do. You need it – and so do I,' Max told her firmly. 'So you felt like a change? I wonder if you can possibly imagine how I felt,' he said, 'left high and dry like that. I racked my brain – night after night I went over and over every single conversation we ever had for some clue as to what I'd done wrong.' He shook his head. 'I know there were one or two areas we didn't see eye to eye on, but nothing that couldn't have been ironed out. But to go off into the blue like that...' He quoted her hastily scribbled note: *Don't try to find me. It's no good. I won't come back.* God, Bryony! Do you have any idea how much that hurt?'

Cornered, she met his eyes, her own guarded and defensive. 'Hurt? Your pride, you mean?' He made no reply, but the reproach in his eyes told her the remark was unworthy and she felt ashamed. She lowered her eyes. 'I'm sorry, that was uncalled-for.'

The barman arrived with their brandies, unloading them from his tray with a smile and a flourish. Bryony took a sip of hers, grateful for its fiery astringence burning her throat. After two more sips she felt a little calmer.

'So – we've established that you wanted to start a new life.' Max had thrown back his brandy in one draught and put the empty glass down on the table. He obviously had no intention of giving up. 'Marriage to me quite clearly wasn't new enough! Obviously you'd fallen out of love with me, but even so, didn't I even rate an explanation?'

'I couldn't explain, Max! I *still* can't! Please don't ask me!' She shook her head, near to the end of her tether. 'I suppose in a way I was – ill. It's true. You're welcome to ask Alison if you don't believe me! I can promise you she'll confirm it.' Her eyes were dark with pain as she looked at him. 'Don't you think I would have explained if I could? Do you think I *wanted* to run away like that? Can you really believe I'd fallen out of love with you? It's not true – any of it.'

'What else was I to believe, damn it?' Max watched with dismay as her eyes brimmed with tears that began to spill over and slide unchecked down her cheeks. He had driven her too hard. Shooting a sideways glance at the barman, he was relieved to see him deep in conversation with a couple who had just come in. Silently he reached into his pocket and passed her a clean white handkerchief. 'Here, have this. I'm sorry, Bryony, I didn't want to upset you. Look, let's get out of here.'

Standing on the pavement outside, she breathed deeply of the warm summer evening and looked at him unhappily. 'I'd like to go home now – Jane will be wondering where I've got to. I said half an hour.'

He nodded, his mouth a tight, grim line. 'Of course.'

She was settling herself into the passenger seat of the car when he suddenly said to her: 'At least explain one thing, Bryony – why did you try to alter your appearance so drastically? When I first saw you I hardly recognised you. Drab clothes, no make-up – your hair.'

'All part of the change of image, I suppose,' she said in a small voice.

He looked unconvinced. 'One thing more – Geoff Mason. Is that serious?'

She shook her head. 'Not in the way you mean.'

He turned to look at her. 'In *what* way, then?'

'We're friends. He's a very kind and understanding person.'

Max gave a short, ironic laugh. 'He'd *have* to be!'

Bryony turned on him. 'I don't really see that it's any of your business, anyway! Would you like me to start asking questions about Sara Daneman?'

He shot her a surprised, mystified look. 'Sara? What about her?'

'You seem to be serious about *her*, that's all.'

Max stared at her. 'What are you talking about? Who says so?'

'You took her home for the weekend, didn't you? It's what everyone thinks, not just me.'

He threw back his head and laughed. 'Hospitals! They're all the same, aren't they? Hotbeds of gossip! Sara and I are family friends from way back – I told you that.'

Bryony shrugged. 'Please don't think you have to explain to me. I was just…'

'*Bryony.*' He reached out to cup her chin, turning her face towards him to search her eyes in the dimness of the car. 'Please, let's stop all this. Just tell me one last thing – truthfully, if possible. Was it true what you said, about not falling out of love with me?'

She felt as though all the resistance had seeped out of her like sawdust from a battered rag doll. Had she actually said that? Back in the bar she had scarcely known what she was saying. But as she met his gaze she knew that she couldn't deny it; on this subject at least she could tell him nothing but the truth. 'It was true,' she admitted.

In the dimness his eyes looked almost luminous. 'And now?'

'That's not fair!' She tried in vain to disengage herself and move away, but his hands were firm on her shoulders as he drew her close, his eyes burning into hers.

'I never got you out of my system, Bryony,' he whispered huskily. 'Oh, don't think I didn't try. I did my very best to hate you – I told myself you weren't worth all the *angst* and the sleepless nights. I believed it too – or I thought I did, until I saw you again. And the fact that you looked like – like Little Orphan Annie only made it worse somehow.' In the dim light of the car his eyes looked angry. 'I knew then that I'd been fighting a losing battle. It's like breathing – something that's part of me, whether I damn well like it or not.'

His mouth came down on hers abruptly. At first she could feel his anger and resentment burning into her own lips like a brand, then the kiss softened and deepened and it was as though a spring of longing was released somewhere deep inside her. She allowed her body to melt against him; winding her arms around his neck, she clung to him, overwhelmed by the love she too had tried so hard to extinguish. They clung to each other like drowning souls, kissing, whispering each other's names, until at last Bryony broke free. 'I – I must go home now,' she whispered breathlessly.

'In a minute. I promise I'll take you in a minute.' Max rubbed his forehead against hers and took both her hands, holding them tightly against his chest. 'Can't you tell me now why you left like that, Bryony?' he begged. 'Surely it can't be so difficult.'

She stirred uncomfortably. Nothing had really changed. Max still loved and wanted her, and that was wonderful – a miracle she had never dared to dream of. And yet in a way it made things even more difficult. If he knew – if he should ever discover the truth, he must surely feel repulsion and loathing for her, and she couldn't face that – not now. 'It's as I said, Max,' she told him haltingly. 'I had a kind of – breakdown. I hardly knew what I was doing at the time. I only knew I had to get away.'

He looked into her eyes anxiously. 'What could have caused it? Haven't you any idea?'

She shook her head. 'Who knows? The pressure of studying hard – all our wedding plans – I suppose it must have been too much.'

He shook his head. 'Poor darling, if only I'd known!' He kissed her. 'I wish you'd been able to tell me. But everything will be all right now.' He smiled down at her. 'Are you happy?'

'Yes.' She pressed her cheek against his.

'I can hardly believe it.' He held her close again, stroking her hair. 'We have so much lost time to make up. The devil of it is that I'm off on another course next week; this time on forensics – but as soon as I get back…' He looked at his watch and gave an exclamation of surprise. 'Good God, I hadn't realised it was as late as that! I'd better get you home before they send out a search party!'

When Max delivered Bryony back at the flat the party was over. They found Jane tidying up, piling dirty plates on to a tray and emptying ashtrays into a cardboard box. Max offered to stay and help, but Bryony assured him that they could cope better alone. When he had gone she fetched another tray from the kitchen and began to help Jane.

The other girl was strangely silent, obviously displeased, and after a few minutes of working in silence Bryony said: 'I'm sorry, Jane, I didn't mean to go and leave you with all the work. Look, why don't you go to bed? I'll finish the rest.'

'It isn't that!' Jane spun round, her cheeks flaming. 'I think you know damned well it's not that! I've had a shock this evening. I didn't know you were that sort of person!'

Bryony stared at her. 'What sort of person?'

'You left Geoff high and dry and went swanning off with Max – *Sara's* boyfriend. You took advantage of the fact that she couldn't come. I call that underhanded.'

Bryony sighed. 'Oh dear. I can see now that it must have looked bad, Jane. But I promise you Geoff understood – really he did. It wasn't the way it looked.'

'No? Which way *was* it, then?' Jane stood facing her, her blue eyes blazing.

Bryony put down her tray. 'First, Max and Sara are just childhood friends, that's all. Secondly, Max and I aren't mere acquaintances. We've known each other a very long time. We trained at the same hospital – when I was nursing.'

Very slowly Jane sat down. The fire went out of her eyes as the truth slowly dawned on her. 'Oh no! You're not trying to tell me that it was *you* he was engaged to, are you?' she said. When Bryony nodded she went on: 'You mean *you* were the one who's accused of breaking his heart and putting him off women for life?'

'I'm afraid so, yes. Only that wasn't quite the way it seemed either,' Bryony told her.

'I don't suppose it was. These things never are,' said Jane almost to herself. She looked up at Bryony. 'Oh *hell!* I seem to have put my foot in it good and proper! Poor Bryony, you must have hated me, saying all those things – passing on all that gossip! I wish you'd said something – letting me rattle on like that.' She looked at Bryony. 'I take it Sara doesn't know either – that it was you, I mean?'

Bryony shook her head. 'No one knows, except Geoff, and he guessed when we ran into Max and Sara that evening and he saw my reaction. I'd appreciate it if you kept it to yourself too.'

'Of course. Naturally.' Jane stood up and crossed the room to hug her friend. 'I'm sorry, love. Sara must have been telling the truth when she said there was nothing in it. Serves me right for jumping to conclusions.' She sighed. 'So what's happened now? Is it all on between you two again?'

'I wouldn't say that exactly,' said Bryony cautiously. 'Let's just say that it could develop again. We'll have to see how things work out.'

'Fantastic!' Jane looked round. 'I'm sure there's some wine left. If we can find a couple of clean glasses we'll drink to it!' She turned in the doorway. 'Bet you're glad I made you wear that dress this evening, aren't you?'

Bryony looked down at the red dress. 'It certainly seems to have brought me luck, doesn't it?' she said. But in her heart she wondered just what *kind* of luck.

On Monday Bryony spent all morning at Fenning House. In the kitchen the residents were preparing a special lunch. Only two more weeks and six of them would be assessed for independence, and this was part of their dummy run. If they passed their tests they would be allocated one of the new flats for the disabled that had recently been opened in the town centre.

There was an air of excitement as they moved to and fro between worktops and cooker, each with his or her own tasks. Peter was peeling vegetables. Bryony made sure that everyone was occupied, then went across to him.

'I hear that Wednesday's your big day,' she said quietly.

His expression as he glanced up at her told her how apprehensive he was.

'I don't know why I'm bothering with this,' he said glumly. 'I'll probably be in hospital now when they come to test us. If this op doesn't work I shall be back to square one this time next week!'

Bryony touched his arm. 'Peter, you don't have to have it, you know. No one can force you.'

He turned on her, his face red and his eyes bright and sharp. 'Oh, for God's sake! I wish you wouldn't keep on saying that!' he snapped. 'On one side I've got Dr Capes and Dr Anderson implying that it's a chance I can't afford to pass up – then there's you saying I needn't have it. Who *do* I believe? I'm going to be the loser either way, if you ask me!' He threw down the potato knife and struggled to manoeuvre his wheelchair, heading for the door. Bryony watched him

181

helplessly, biting her lip.

'What's up with him, then?'

She turned to see Dave Freeman at her elbow. 'He's upset and worried about his op next week,' she told him. 'I think I said the wrong thing.'

Dave grunted: 'Huh! Who can say the *right* thing? He's been impossible lately. "*Shall* I have it? *Shan't* I have it?" I bloody well know what I'd do, given half a chance *I* might get to walk again. But I should have his luck!'

'You do have a mum and dad, though, Dave,' she reminded him gently. 'It's all right trying for independence when you know you have a family to fall back on. Peter has no one to advise him and no one to support him if things go wrong.'

He looked up at her in surprise. 'Go wrong? I thought this op had a pretty good success rate. They wouldn't chance it if it hadn't – would they?'

'All surgery carries its own risks,' she told him. 'There are no gilt-edged guarantees. Peter has coped so well. He was even beginning to accept his disability psychologically. This time next week he could have been declared fit to move into a flat and cope on his own...' She spread her hands, seeing that she was getting her point across to Dave.

'Yeah – I see what you mean,' he said, nodding his head. He turned to the worktop where his apple pie was awaiting its crust. 'Look, I'll just get that in the oven, then I'll pop along and have a word with him, eh?'

Bryony smiled. 'That would be nice, Dave. I'm sure he'd appreciate it. I'll keep an eye on your pie and make sure it doesn't burn.'

Dave's particular brand of wry humour must have done the trick. When the cooking session was over and the drama group assembled in the recreation hall, Peter was there in his usual place, ready to take charge of the tape recorder. Today they were ready to make the finished recording of their play and everyone was keyed up and looking forward to the prospect. Even though Bryony assured them that any mistakes could be edited out of the recording afterwards, each of them was keen to get his or her part perfect first time.

As she bent to check that the tape recorder was switched on she felt a light touch on her shoulder and looked up to see Peter smiling ruefully at her.

'I wish we could edit out some of the things we say, Bryony,' he told her shyly. 'I'm finding myself wishing it more and more lately. I'm sorry I bit your head off.'

She smiled warmly at him. 'No need to apologise. If I were you I'd be absolute hell to live with,' she told him. 'As for what you said – consider it edited!'

Dropping in at the office with her reports at lunchtime, Bryony ran into Alison as she was coming out of her office. The older woman's eyes lit up when she saw her niece.

'Bryony! I'm so glad I've seen you. I was just off for a bite of lunch. Come with me?' Bryony hesitated and her aunt sighed. 'Oh, come on. You're not still cross with me, are you? Do come, and I'd like to talk to you about the wedding. It's only a week on Saturday, so there's no time to be lost.'

'Oh, well, in that case...' Bryony allowed her aunt to take her arm and steer her towards the canteen, Alison chatting brightly all the way about outfits and where to go for the week's honeymoon she and Graham were planning.

When they were settled at their table Alison said: 'I'd like you to be my bridesmaid. Will you? It's only a register office wedding, but we thought it would be nice to do it properly with a best man and everything.'

Bryony smiled. 'I'd like that very much, Alison. And I'm really happy for you, you know that, don't you?'

'Of course I do.' For a few minutes they discussed outfits, then Alison said: 'I was wondering if there was anyone you'd like to invite yourself?'

'Me? Why should I...?' Bryony drew a deep breath. 'Ah, the grapevine has been buzzing again, then?'

Alison affected an innocent expression. 'Not at all. It's just that I happened to be talking to Geoff Mason. He told me about the party you and Jane gave. He mentioned the fact that Max was there and that you and he – well...'

Bryony sighed. Max was right, there was nothing one could keep secret around a hospital. 'Yes. We met and – talked,' she said guardedly.

Alison looked at her niece. 'No doubt he asked questions. What did you tell him? I only ask so that I can corroborate your story if necessary,' she added quickly.

'That I had a kind of breakdown,' Bryony told her. 'It was as close to the truth as I'm prepared to go.' The note of finality in her voice brought the subject to a close. She felt reluctant to talk any more about what had passed between herself and Max on the night of the party. In a desperate effort to change the subject she asked: 'How is your – how is the patient you told me about?'

'Glenys, you mean?' Alison tried not to show her eagerness. 'The girl from the VES?'

'Yes – that one.'

'She's still in the hospital,' Alison told her. 'Up in Neuro. She had a suspected skull fracture that was causing concern, you see – apart from all the other injuries.' She paused, trying to assess Bryony's mood, but the veiled eyes told her nothing. 'I've seen quite a lot of her, actually,' she went on cautiously, 'but I'm afraid she still won't talk, either to me or the nice young policewoman who's been to see her. There's a good case for "grievous bodily harm" alone, and we were hoping we might at least get a description of the man...'

'You can't possibly imagine she'd want to *remember* what the man looked like?' Bryony snapped. 'Don't you see – all she wants is to forget!'

'That's precisely where I believe you could help us,' said Alison quietly. 'No one would understand as you do. I believe you'd know instinctively what to ask and how to phrase it.'

'No!' Bryony laid down her knife and fork. 'I'm still trying to come to terms with my own experience. How could I help? Anyway, I don't think she should be put through all that. I don't agree with any of it.'

'Because you've got a block about it, Bryony!' Alison said sharply. 'And you're never going to come to terms with it until you break down that barrier. Help someone else and you might stand a chance of doing that.'

'I *am* coping!' insisted Bryony, her teeth clenched. 'I *am!*'

'Rubbish! You can't even say the word, can you – well, *can* you?' Alison leaned forward across the table. 'I've noticed repeatedly. Attack, ordeal, *experience* even. Never rape!'

Bryony leapt to her feet, the room spinning round her. *'Stop it!'*

'Sit down, Bryony,' Alison said wearily. 'For heaven's sake, don't let's have all this again. You brought the subject up, not me. Look, I won't mention it again. From now on it's a closed chapter. Let's talk about the wedding. Damn it all, you're the only family I've got. I don't want to lose you.'

Bryony sat down again, partly because of Alison's plea and partly because her legs felt as though they wouldn't have carried her more than a couple of yards. But although she allowed Alison to jolly her into a discussion about outfits for the coming wedding, the evil, half-remembered nightmare remained to haunt the corners of her mind, like a suffocating blanket or a cloud of poisonous gas.

CHAPTER NINE

Peter Gardner's operation was scheduled for ten-thirty on Wednesday morning, and as Bryony went about her morning routine she found her mind returning to him again and again. Glancing at her watch as she stopped her car outside the Grimshaws' neat little terraced house in Bridge Street, she saw that it was just five to ten. She sat for a moment, thinking of Peter – imagining how he must be feeling as they prepared him and wheeled him up to the theatre. Mercifully the pre-med would have calmed his fears but, knowing Peter as she did, she knew he would still be anxious.

She had promised him she would go to visit him later, when she called in at the hospital at the end of her day's work. Perhaps she would see Max there too. The thought came unexpectedly into her mind and sent a frisson of excitement tingling through her. She hadn't seen Max since the night of the party. The forensics course he had been on had taken him up to Tuesday evening. She had half hoped he might ring her last night. She had made up her mind to ask him to Alison and Graham's wedding – if he did get in touch again. Of course, there was always the chance that he might have had second thoughts and decided there was no point in seeing her again. That was something she had braced herself to face.

She found Mr Grimshaw in good spirits. Above the fireplace in the small cosy living room hung a simple but effective watercolour painting of a snow scene. Mrs Grimshaw pointed to it proudly.

'There, just look at that, Miss Slade. What do you think of it?'

'Is it really one of yours?' Bryony turned to her patient, who was trying very hard to keep the smile of achievement off his craggy face.

'It is that,' he told her. 'Never was one to be beaten. I'm doing an oil as well, but that takes longer to dry, you know.'

'And Geoff Mason tells me you're coming along famously with your physio,' Bryony smiled. 'Before you know it you'll be back on your feet.'

'He *has* been!' Mrs Grimshaw told her triumphantly. 'Mr Mason got him a walking frame and he's been down the garden with it – *twice!*' She lowered her voice: 'With my help, of course.'

'That's great.' Bryony had a sudden idea. 'I wonder...' she said hesitantly. 'My aunt is getting married on Saturday. I don't suppose you could paint her a picture – for me to give her as a wedding present? I want to pay you for it, of course. It'll be your first professional commission.' She looked at him enquiringly. 'Would you do that for me?'

George Grimshaw smiled. 'I should just think not!' he told her indignantly. 'I'll be happy to paint you a picture, but not for money! Not after what you've done for me.' He turned to the table beside him and drew his box of painting things towards him. 'You can call and collect it on Friday evening. I'll make a start right away!'

In the hallway Mrs Grimshaw smiled as she saw Bryony out. 'Mr Mason has done wonders with the physiotherapy,' she said. 'But you know it was the challenge of trying to paint with his left hand that really picked up George's spirits again. Oddly enough, the strength began to come back into his right hand almost immediately.' She laid a hand on Bryony's arm. 'Thank you for asking him to paint a picture for your aunt. It was a lovely thought.'

'I meant it,' Bryony assured her. 'I can't think of a nicer present for her. I know she'll be delighted with it.'

That afternoon at Dunster House the matron told Bryony that Annie Herd had moved in the previous Friday. She confessed that she was a little worried about the old lady, as she seemed withdrawn, and after Bryony had made her round of the elderly residents, she went to visit her, knocking gently on the door of her room and putting her head round it.

'Hello, Annie, may I come in?'

Annie's face lit up and she struggled hurriedly to her feet. 'How nice to see you, love. Wait a minute, I'll put the kettle on. You can stay to have a cuppa with me, can't you?'

Bryony looked at her watch. It was half past four. 'Well, all right,' she said. 'Just a quick one.' Annie looked pleased and busied herself, putting out cups and saucers and plugging in her electric kettle. 'How are you settling in, Annie?' asked Bryony. 'Have you made friends? I expected to see you in the lounge or the TV room.'

Annie pulled a face. 'I've got my own telly

– and there's no need for you to worry about me having nothing to do. I've still got my crochet.' She held up the fine shawl she was making, smiling mischievously at Bryony. 'Look, it's growing. You'll have to hurry up and find that Mr Right, or the baby's shawl will be ready before you are!' Her frail shoulders shook with laughter.

'But I thought you'd enjoy the company here,' Bryony told her. 'It's much more cheerful than in the hospital. Don't you want to mix?'

Annie pulled a face. 'What do I want with a lot of old fogies?' she said scornfully. 'I don't *feel* old – not that old, anyway. I like young folks like you.'

Bryony sat down and took the cup that Annie handed to her. 'All right, you don't have to mix if you don't want to. That's the point of having your own room.' She took a sip of her tea. 'But have you thought that the others might have felt exactly the same as you once? Don't you think you're judging them by appearances? If you got to know them you might be surprised at how interesting they are.'

Annie shook her head. 'I've heard them at mealtimes. All they talk about is the past. It's like there's no future! Either that or they're boasting about how much money their sons and daughters have got and how clever their grandchildren are.'

'We all have to justify our existence,' Bryony told her. 'It's just a way of letting others know that we haven't lived empty lives. I'm sure they'd like to hear about your life too.' She smiled. 'You're probably arousing a lot of curiosity right at this moment, being the latest arrival. If you shut yourself away in here and keep them guessing they'll be making up stories about you.'

Annie chuckled delightedly. 'Annie the beautiful Russian spy,' she said wickedly. 'Well, if they want to think that, let 'em. It'll keep their minds off their arthritis for once, won't it?'

Before she left Dunster House Bryony had extracted a promise from Annie to try to be more sociable, though she guessed that in spite of the old lady's protests her main trouble was mere shyness.

As she came out of the office after writing out the day's reports she stood for a moment in the corridor, apprehension suddenly stirring in the pit of her stomach. The day had been a busy one. Once she had started there had scarcely been time to worry about Peter, but now the moment had come when she would find out how successful, or otherwise, the surgery to his spine had been. She wondered briefly how she would face him if it had been unsuccessful. Taking a deep breath, she walked resolutely to the lift and pressed the button for the fifth floor and Men's Surgical.

Sister told her she could look in on Peter for five minutes. 'He's in one of the side wards for the moment,' she said. 'And still rather woozy from the anaesthetic. The op was a long one, but Mr Keller has been to see him since he came back from theatre and he's very pleased.'

'It was a success, then?' Bryony asked hopefully.

Sister pursed her lips. 'We'll have to see,' she said guardedly. 'But it appears that Mr Keller was able to ease the pressure on the peripheral nerves, which is bound to improve things. Time will tell just how much improvement there is.'

Looking into the small room, Bryony found Peter dozing. Slipping inside, she drew up a chair and sat quietly at his bedside.

After a moment or two he opened his eyes and looked at her, smiling drowsily. 'Hello.

Are you really there, or am I dreaming?' he asked.

She touched his hand. 'I'm really here, Peter. How do you feel?'

'Groggy,' he admitted. 'I can't seem to tell what's real and what isn't.'

'That's the anaesthetic,' she told him. 'Are you in any pain?'

'No.' He looked at her, suddenly alert. 'Have they said anything to you? Do you know whether...?'

'It looks promising, Peter,' she told him quietly. 'From what I hear Mr Keller is pleased with you. But you'll have to ask the consultant or Dr Anderson for more details when he comes to see you tomorrow.' She squeezed his fingers gently and stood up. 'Sister said five minutes only. You must rest now. I'm glad it's all over and you're all right. I'll see you tomorrow. Goodbye.'

''Bye, Bryony – and thanks – for coming.' Already his eyelids were drooping again, and when she turned in the doorway to look back at him he was asleep.

Bryony thanked Sister for letting her visit and made her way back along the corridor. As she got out of the lift on the ground floor she almost collided with Max, who was getting in. He grasped her shoulders to

196

steady her.

'Steady! Where's the fire?'

She looked up at him. 'Oh – hello.'

He smiled. 'I was going to ring you last night, but it was late when I got in.'

'It's all right.' There was a pause, then she said: 'I've been to see Peter. He seems fine.'

'Yes…'

He glanced up as the lift doors began to close and Bryony said quickly: 'Don't let me keep you.'

Max shook his head. 'It doesn't matter. Look, come and have a cup of tea – if you've time, that is.'

She blushed with pleasure. 'I've finished work. Tea would be nice.'

They went to the visitors' cafeteria in the hospital entrance hall. It was quiet at this time of the day and they found a table in the corner. Max put the tray down on the table and passed her one of the cups. 'Peter's op went very well. Jon Keller was satisfied that he'd done all he could.'

'Oh – that has an ominous ring!'

He looked up in surprise. 'On the contrary, he was optimistic, but you know what these cases are like. We'll just have to wait and see. Jon has suggested a spell at Stoke Mandeville. But it's early days for that kind of decision.'

Bryony nodded, stirring her tea. 'And your course – how was it?'

'Fine. Very interesting. I promised to go home next weekend and tell Dad all about it. Obviously he's fascinated by all the new technology.'

'Oh.' Bryony's heart plummeted. That ruled out asking him to Alison's wedding.

'What is it? Have I said something?' He was looking at her enquiringly.

'Oh, no.' She managed a smile. 'It was just that I had an invitation to pass on, but if you've made other arrangements.'

'Might I know what the invitation is?' He smiled.

'Alison is getting married,' she told him. 'My aunt Alison – I believe you know her slightly. She's marrying Graham White. He's an occupational psychologist here at the City.' She moistened her suddenly dry lips. 'I mentioned that we – that you came to Jane's party and she suggested you might like to come to the wedding, if you were free. But you're not, so it doesn't matter.'

'Wait a minute!' laughed Max. 'Don't write me off like that. When is the wedding?'

'On Saturday morning, ten-thirty at the register office, followed by a small buffet lunch – just a few friends and colleagues from here.'

'Well, I don't see why I shouldn't accept,' he said. 'It fits in quite well, as it happens. I wasn't going home until the afternoon anyway. Bryony...' His hand covered hers on the table. 'As a matter of fact I was about to ask you to come home with me afterwards. It would just be till Sunday evening. How about it?'

Bryony felt her cheeks burn with sudden colour. She shrank back into her chair, shaking her head. 'Oh, no, I couldn't do that?'

He frowned. 'Why not? I'm sure Dad and Aunt Lou would be pleased to see you.'

'I can't believe that,' she said unhappily. 'Not after what happened.'

He sighed. 'That was all a very long time ago, Bryony.'

'Time doesn't erase what happened – nothing can ever do that,' she said, half to herself.

He touched her hand again. 'A new start was what I had in mind, Bryony,' he said softly. 'And there's no better place to make a new start than back at the beginning, so what do you say?' His eyes looked into hers and she felt herself reaching out to him. But it was as though something held her back. How could she tell him how much she dreaded going back to that place with all its nightmare associations; facing his father and aunt? After what Aunt Lou said to Sara it was clear that she at least had never forgiven her – and there was nothing she could say in her own defence; no explanation she could offer.

Looking up at Max, seeing in his eyes how much he wanted her to go, she steeled herself to make the decision. If it was possible to block off the past, convince herself it had never happened, then she must try. If it meant that she and Max could make a new start then it was worth the effort, however much it might cost her. Slowly she nodded, her mouth so dry she could barely say the words: 'All right, Max. I'd like to go.'

'Great! I'll ring and let them know. And I'd love to go to the wedding. Will you thank your aunt for the invitation? I'll pick you up on Saturday morning. Ten o'clock be all right?'

'Fine.' She smiled, trying to look pleased – trying to shake off the feeling that she had burned a vital bridge.

Bryony woke early on Saturday morning and lay for a moment, drowsily thinking of the day ahead. Then she remembered the impending visit to the Andersons' and her heart sank with apprehension. Through the gap in the curtains she could see the sky; a clear hazy blue that promised a fine, warm day. For Alison's sake she must try to put her own anxieties aside.

She got up and showered, then, in her dressing gown, she padded to the kitchen to make tea and toast. She laid a tray and took Jane her breakfast in bed. The other girl sat up, blinking in surprise.

'What's all this? I thought only brides got breakfast in bed. You're not mixing me up with Alison, are you?'

'No, I couldn't sleep, so I got up early and thought I'd give you a treat.'

Jane leaned back against the pillows, sighing luxuriously as she sipped her tea. 'This is the life all right! Just my rotten luck I had to be on duty to-day. I'd have loved to have gone to the wedding. Still...' she grinned mischievously, 'you won't miss me – not when you've got Max Anderson to escort you!' She peered at her friend. 'You look a bit peaky. What is it? The thought of this weekend visit giving you the collywobbles?'

Bryony nodded. 'Max's family never really approved of me. And after what happened I can hardly expect them to welcome me with open arms, can I?'

Jane nodded. 'I can imagine how you must feel. Still, you might get a surprise. They might even have a conscience about the way they treated you. These cases are never the fault of only *one* person, are they?' She glanced at the bedside clock. 'Oh lord, look at the time! I'll have to get up or I'll be late.'

The flat seemed very empty when Jane had gone. Bryony washed up and made the beds, wandered round with a duster and vacuumed the carpets. She wrapped up the watercolour painting she had collected from George Grimshaw the previous evening. It was an idyllic woodland scene and she knew Alison would love it, especially when she knew its history.

When she had finished she was surprised to find that all the jobs she had done had taken her less than an hour. There was still an hour and a half before Max would be here to pick her up. As she passed the telephone her fingers reached out to hover over it. For a second she hesitated, then, making up her mind, she lifted the receiver and dialled Alison's number.

'Hello?' Alison sounded her usual brisk self.

'Hello. It's me – Bryony. I wondered how you were feeling?'

'I'm fine.'

'Not nervous?'

Alison laughed at the other end of the line. 'I've known Graham for years. Why should I be nervous?'

'I don't know – wedding nerves, perhaps. Alison...' Bryony twisted the telephone flex between her fingers. 'Max is coming to the wedding. He – asked me to go home with him afterwards, for the weekend.'

'I see. And...?'

'I've said I'll go.'

'And now you wish you hadn't?'

'It's going to be an ordeal,' Bryony admitted. 'I haven't been back there since...'

Alison sighed audibly. 'Oh, Bryony! If you want to know what I think – and I take it that's why you're ringing – I think it's the best thing that could happen. You've got to face up to it sooner or later. Whether you like it or not, Max is all part of what happened to you, and until you get it all out into the open...'

Mentally Bryony switched off. She might have known what Alison's reaction would be. Why had she bothered to ask? She had no right to bother her on her wedding day anyway. When her aunt's voice had stopped talking she said: 'Thanks, Alison, I'm sure you're right. Don't worry about me. See you at the register office – goodbye.' She was just replacing the receiver when she heard Alison's voice speaking again:

'Bryony, you do still have your key to the flat, I take it?'

'Yes. I'll give it back to you later if you remind me.'

'No, keep it. I'd like you to keep an eye on the flat while Graham and I are away. Will you do that?'

'Of course.' As she replaced the receiver, Bryony reflected wryly that Alison's ordered mind was never far away from the practicalities of life. Ah well, that's the psychologist in her, she reminded herself.

The outfit Bryony had chosen for the wedding was of a soft delphinium blue, a dress and matching hip-length jacket, flatteringly cut to accentuate her slim figure. On Jane's instructions she had applied a careful make-up and flicked up the soft, dark hair that framed her face in the new gamin style that everyone had complimented her on since the night of Jane's party. When she was ready she took a long look at herself in the bedroom mirror. She had grown so used to the drab image she had adopted four years ago that the vitally attractive young woman who looked back at her from the mirror seemed like a stranger. It was an odd feeling – like looking at herself through the wrong end of a telescope. She felt almost as though the old Bryony were being left behind in the wardrobe with her old clothes. But she had little time to ponder on this idea, for the doorbell shrilled, jerking her out of her reverie. Max was here!

When she opened the door and he saw her for the first time he caught his breath. There was a new vibrant loveliness about her. The outfit she wore seemed to sing with colour, reminding him poignantly of the Bryony he had fallen in love with and lost so long ago; the young girl whose bright, clear eyes had none of the haunted look they wore all too often now.

He stepped inside the small hallway. 'You look beautiful,' he told her simply.

She blushed. 'Thank you.' There was something about his eyes as they held hers that momentarily disturbed her. She stepped backwards away from him as he reached out a hand to her. 'I've packed an overnight case. It's in the living room – and Alison's present. We'd better go or we'll be late.'

In the car on the way to the register office she chattered brightly, telling him about George Grimshaw's picture. 'I'd already bought them another present, of course,' she told him. 'A dinner service. This is something extra. I wanted George to have a proper commission, you see.'

Max was silent, sensing her unease – guessing at the reason for it. The wedding went without a hitch. Alison looked radiant and beautiful in a cream silk two-piece. There was a lump in Bryony's throat as she saw the look the couple exchanged when the registrar pronounced them man and wife. They had waited so long. They truly deserved their happiness.

The buffet lunch, which was held at the couple's favourite restaurant, was attended by all Alison's colleagues who hadn't been able to squeeze into the register office. Bryony already knew most of them by sight. At the buffet table Joan Medworth, a social worker, was in earnest conversation with Alison, and at one point Bryony caught the name *Glenys*. Her blood froze as she realised who they were talking about and she turned away hurriedly, but not before she had heard Joan say that the girl had been discharged.

Bryony retreated into a corner and sipped her drink. She couldn't help imagining how the girl Glenys must be feeling. Had she anyone to turn to, she wondered, any support now that she was alone? Joan looked kind and caring, but she would have so many other cases to worry about.

'Penny for them?'

She looked up to see Geoff standing watching her. She smiled. 'I was miles away,' she confessed.

'I could see that!' He raised an eyebrow at her. 'How are things?' He nodded towards Max, who had gone to refill their glasses. 'It's good to see you two together.'

Bryony smiled at him. 'Thanks. Are you with anyone?'

Geoff laughed. 'You bet! Sara was at a loose end, so we teamed up and came along together.' He pointed across the room to where Sara stood, talking to a doctor colleague. She looked stunning in a jade green dress. Catching them looking, she waved cheerily. Bryony was relieved; she had half expected Sara to be resentful about the way Max had stopped asking her out.

'We're going to Max's home for the

weekend,' she confided to Geoff. 'At the moment I'm terrified at the thought.'

'Ah, so that's why you were looking so pensive!' Geoff patted her shoulder. 'Stop worrying, you'll be fine. Good luck, love. You deserve it.'

Toasts were drunk, telegrams read and speeches made, and in no time at all they were waving the newlyweds off to an undisclosed destination. Then, and only then, did Bryony's mind return to the weekend ahead. She turned to look at Max, a moment of blind panic suddenly seizing her. If only she could think of some way to escape – to get out of it. But she knew that it was something that had to be faced. If she and Max were going to start seeing each other seriously again she would have to meet his family again eventually.

The drive took just under two hours and Bryony was quiet for most of the way, scarcely noticing the scenery as it rushed past. But as they reached the coast road and she caught her first glimpse of the slate-blue strip of sea, her heart gave an involuntary leap. Eagerly she wound down the car window and took a deep breath. Already she could smell the sea's tang on the salty air.

In the distance gulls wheeled and dipped,

but here, in the peace of the Norfolk marshes, the sweeter song of a lark reached her. Looking up for the source of the song, she saw him, a tiny speck hovering high in a clear blue sky above the waving grasses. She sighed. The scene brought back so many nostalgic memories. She had once been so happy in this lovely place – before everything had changed. Before that moment of mindless brutality had shattered her life and changed her whole personality.

Max smiled. 'It never changes, does it? The one thing you can always rely on.' He turned to look at her. 'You've been very quiet. Are you going to miss Alison?'

Bryony's thoughts were so vivid that she was almost surprised he hadn't shared them. 'No. I daresay I shall see just as much of her as I did before.' She recognised that he was really asking the reason for her preoccupation, but she made no attempt to supply an excuse. How could she?

It was five-thirty when they finally arrived in the picturesque Norfolk village of East Keel. They drove past the pond on the outskirts of the village where the ducks quacked a noisy welcome; past the huddle of rosy brick and shingle cottages and the church with its squat, square tower, then finally into the tree-lined drive of Arden House, the Andersons' comfortable home. Bryony's heart was beating fast as Max sounded the horn and brought the car to a halt at the front door.

Almost immediately it opened and Dr James Anderson came out on to the steps to greet them. Bryony saw that he hadn't changed; a little greyer perhaps and maybe slightly heavier, but the warm brown eyes that were so like Max's were the same as ever. He grasped his son's hand and shook it warmly.

'You've made good time! Come along in.' He turned to Bryony, who stood diffidently by. 'Bryony, my dear – after all this time!' He held out both hands and when she put her own into them he pulled her towards him and bent to kiss her cheek warmly. 'When Max told us he'd found you again I could hardly believe it. Just what Louise would call "fate"! Come along in. You must be tired after the drive.'

Bryony was touched by the warmth of his welcome, and as they followed him into the hall Max touched her hand and gave her a smile and the ghost of a wink as though to reassure her.

As they stood in the hall Louise Anderson

came through from the kitchen. She hugged Max, then turned to Bryony, but where James's eyes had been warm her own were cool and guarded.

'How nice to see you after so long, Bryony,' she said politely. 'If you'll come with me I'll show you your room.' She took Bryony's small case from Max and walked ahead of them up the wide staircase.

Bryony had been given the guest room at the back of the house, overlooking the old walled garden. The windows were open and through them drifted the scent of summer flowers; roses, pinks and scented stocks. She breathed in its evocative deliciousness. 'Oh, how lovely!' She turned to the older woman. 'It's good of you to make me so welcome.'

Louise Anderson was busying herself turning back the bed. Now she straightened her back and looked directly at Bryony for the first time. 'You won't hurt him again, will you?' she said bluntly.

The question was like a sharp slap, and it took Bryony a moment to recover from its impact. 'No,' she said at last. 'I won't. I didn't want – didn't *mean* to hurt him before, you know.'

Louise's mouth tightened and she made a move towards the door. Halfway across the room she stopped and turned, and now Bryony saw something else in her eyes. Now there was doubt and uncertainty. 'I – have to know one thing,' she said. 'I'm not asking anything else – not prying…' She swallowed hard. 'Did *I* have anything to do with it? Was it – was it *my* fault?'

Bryony's eyes flew open in surprise. '*Your* fault?' she echoed. 'Why should you think that?'

The older woman licked her lips, the palms of her hands rubbing against the sides of her skirt. 'I – don't know.' Her eyes met Bryony's and she shook her head impatiently. 'No, that's not true. If I'm honest I *do* know why I think it. It's tortured me ever since that morning, when Max came and told us the wedding was off – read your note to us.' She sat down on the edge of the bed. 'I wasn't very nice to you, was I?' She didn't wait for a reply but hurried on: 'It's true. I didn't even try to make you feel one of the family. I was always hinting – making spiteful remarks when I knew you couldn't retaliate. I was the archetypal "mother-in-law"! The sort that comedians make jokes about.' She gave a bitter little laugh. 'Who ever heard of a mother-in-law who never had a child? The motives were the same, though. I was jealous. I didn't want to lose him, I suppose.'

Bryony didn't know what to say. She felt sorry for the woman who sat slumped on the bed. She longed to reassure her that it would have taken far more than her jealous jibes to make her turn her back on the man she loved so much. But to reassure her fully she would have to tell her the truth – and that was out of the question. She took a step towards the older woman and touched her shoulder.

'Please don't blame yourself,' she whispered. 'I promise you it was nothing to do with anything you said.' But even as she said the words she heard an echo of Aunt Lou's strident opinionated voice that evening at dinner: *The clothes they wear! They ask for it!* And she knew in that moment that in her own small way Aunt Lou *had* contributed to the decision she had made on that fateful morning, had woven one slim thread into the complicated pattern that had ended in disaster.

She sat down beside Louise. 'It's impossible to say what the reason was,' she said. 'I suppose it was a lot of things. But I can tell you one thing truthfully. It wasn't because I stopped loving Max.'

The older woman turned to look at her. 'And you still love him?'

Bryony nodded. 'Yes.'

A smile of relief lit the other woman's face. 'Oh, I'm so glad! I've blamed myself all this time for the unhappiness. I've prayed so hard that I might have a chance to put it right.' She laid her hand on Bryony's arm. 'I kept your wedding dress, Bryony. It's still hanging there in the wardrobe – and now...'

'Please...' Bryony held up her hand, retreating a little, 'you mustn't expect too much. It's true that I still love Max, but nothing's the same. I don't think it ever can be after all that happened.'

Aunt Lou's eyes clouded. 'What are you trying to tell me?' she asked.

'Just that if anyone is going to be hurt this time, I'm afraid it'll be me,' Bryony told her sadly.

CHAPTER TEN

Dinner that evening was relaxed. Bryony felt as though she had been accepted back into the Anderson household generously and without reservations. Aunt Lou's revelations had surprised her and the older woman certainly seemed to be going out of her way to make her feel welcome. She had cooked a sumptuous dinner and afterwards she wouldn't hear of Bryony helping with the washing up.

'I have help,' she told her as they rose from the table. 'Mrs Jenkins who comes in to help me clean twice a week has promised to look in for half an hour later.'

James nodded his agreement. 'Why don't you come into the study with me, Max, while these two go off and talk clothes or whatever women talk about,' he said. 'Then you can tell me all about your forensics course.'

Aunt Lou shot him a pointed look. 'What an idea, James! Plenty of time for all your shop talk tomorrow. Let these youngsters go off for a walk by themselves. It's a beautiful evening.'

They walked down through the garden, admiring Aunt Lou's herbaceous border, ablaze with colour against the sun-warmed stone of the garden wall. Max opened the gate at the bottom and led her through. They crossed the lane and a few minutes later they were on the dunes, with the sea gleaming in the distance like a silver ribbon. The sky was a deep, soft purple shot with the crimson stain left by the last rays of the sun. They climbed the highest of the dunes and stood with the calm sea below them, gently rattling the pebbles at the water's edge.

Bryony breathed deeply and stretched out her arms. 'Oh – I'd forgotten how beautiful it is here,' she sighed. 'So peaceful. It has a sort of gentle wildness.'

Max looked at her. It was in his mind to tell her that the words she had used might well describe her. She was so different from the confident girl he had known before. Now she reminded him of a half tamed wild creature – timid yet alert, defensive yet vulnerable. He was so afraid of losing her again, of doing something that would frighten her away. If only he knew what had driven her away from him! But some deep instinct told him not to probe too deeply. He slipped an arm around her shoulders and drew her close to his side. 'Do you feel happier now?' he asked. 'Less tense?'

She looked up at him and nodded. 'Yes – much happier. Your father and aunt have been so kind, taking me back into their home again.'

His arm tightened about her. 'Why shouldn't they? They trust me, Bryony,' he said. 'They always knew, just as I did, that there had to be a good reason. I think in our different ways we each felt to blame.'

She shook her head. 'You weren't. At least…' She trailed off, frowning – afraid of tying herself in knots again.

Max took her hand. 'Come on, let's go down to the sea's edge.' He ran down the steep slope of the dune, pulling her with him. Bryony slithered on the dry sand and almost fell. Stumbling after him, she laughed breathlessly.

'Max, wait!'

He stopped abruptly at the water's edge, turning to catch her in his arms. As she leaned against him, gasping for breath, his mouth came down on hers in a long, searching kiss.

'Bryony – oh, Bryony,' he whispered as he crushed her close. 'The times I've walked here alone by the sea and thought of you, wishing you were here with me like this! I can hardly believe it's actually happening.' He kissed her again and she wound her arms around his neck, pressing close, grateful for the lean strength of him; feeling in that moment that everything must surely be all right now that they were together again.

They walked along the beach for a while, arms around each other, then found a sheltered hollow in the heart of a shallow dune. Max sank on to the sand, drawing her down beside him. Stretching out, he eased her hand into the hollow of his shoulder, one arm protectively around her, and for a while they lay there, looking up at the stars. When he moved, rolling over to kiss her, Bryony melted, returning his kisses with a fervour and passion that matched his own, thrilling to the intoxicating sensation of his strong warm hands caressing her; touching her hair and tracing the outline of her features. Trailing down her neck, they paused against the little pulse at the base of her throat, beating out its telltale message for him. Then he kissed her again, more demandingly this time, his lips hard against hers. His voice was husky with tenderness as he whispered her name, his breath caressing her ear. She knew he wanted her, and in that moment she wanted him too, with all her heart and soul. She knew she was telling him so with every beat of her heart against his, every movement of her lips as they parted eagerly for his kiss. Yet the moment she felt his fingers gently unfasten the buttons of her dress, felt his fingers, cool against the warmth of her skin, she grew tense. *This is Max,* she told herself. *This is the man I love and almost lost because – because of...!* Panic gripped her, her throat tightened with a totally irrational fear.

Unable to bear the tension any longer, she pushed him away. 'No, Max! – not now – not here.'

He looked down at her, his eyes dark and luminous as they searched hers. She saw him struggling to understand her sudden withdrawal. After a moment he said: 'Bryony, I think we should try to get away somewhere for a few days.' He sat up, staring out at the sea. 'We need time – time to get to know one another again; time for – rediscovery.'

Bryony was silent, sick with misery. By

rediscovery did he mean time for him to wring the truth about what had happened out of her?'

He looked down at her. 'Will you come? Would you like that?'

'Of course I would,' she said breathlessly. 'It's just that I – don't think I have any more time off due.'

'A weekend, then?'

'Yes – perhaps. I – I don't know.'

Max sighed, pushing a hand through his hair. 'Why do I have the feeling that I've been here before?' He rose to his feet, suddenly impatient.

She scrambled to her feet and hurried after him, her throat tight with tears as she touched his sleeve. 'I didn't mean – it's not like before, Max.'

'No?' His tone was sharp and tense. 'You could have fooled me, Bryony.' He stopped and turned to look at her. 'What *is* it? One minute you're so warm and responsive, making me believe you feel as I do, the next minute you're fighting me off, almost as though I'm trying to…'

'*No!*' Her hand shot out and she covered his mouth with her fingers. 'Please don't say things like that,' she begged, her voice trembling on the edge of tears. 'I'm sorry.'

'I'm sorry too.' He pulled her into his arms and held her gently, his chin resting on the top of her head. 'Are we going to go through life apologising to each other, Bryony?' he asked wearily, his voice thick with despair. 'Apologising without knowing what for?' She made no reply, and after a moment he kissed her forehead gently. 'You're tired,' he said. 'It's been a long day. Let's go back to the house.'

Bryony slept little, and Aunt Lou remarked on her pallor at the breakfast table next morning.

'You must get out in the fresh air today,' she announced. 'I'll pack lunch for you.' She turned to Max. 'Why don't you drive along the coast to Blakeney? There should be plenty of sailing today. It's fun to watch even if you're not taking part.'

But halfway through breakfast the telephone rang. James got up to answer it, but came back into the room a few minutes later.

'Tony Jacobs would like to speak to you,' he told Max. 'He rang to remind me about a meeting up at the hospital tomorrow and when I told him you were here he said he'd like a word.'

Excusing himself, Max left the table and

went into the hall. James smiled at Bryony. 'I don't think you ever met Tony – he came after you left St Hildred's. He's a senior registrar now. He and Max worked together on Jon Keller's firm. Actually Tony took Max's place.'

'Oh, I see.' Bryony felt the first stirrings of apprehension, though she didn't, at that moment, know why.

'Tony was married about two months ago,' Aunt Lou put in, 'to a girl you must have known when you were at St Hildred's. They're still living in one of the hospital flats – waiting for their new house to be finished.'

Max came back into the room, looking pleased. 'We've been invited to lunch with Tony and Jill,' he announced. He began to butter a piece of toast. 'They're both looking forward to seeing you, Bryony. You never knew Tony, but he married Jill – Nurse Trent. She's a Sister now. She was in your year, wasn't she?'

Bryony was silent, panic making her heart race. Of course she knew Jill. They had even shared a room at one point in their training. She would know all about Bryony's sudden disappearance and, no doubt, would want to know the details of it the moment they were together. But it wasn't only that that filled her mind with dread. Going back to St Hildred's; treading the same ground, seeing the same buildings – places. The thought made her shudder with revulsion.

When breakfast was over she walked out into the garden. Max followed her. 'What's wrong?' he asked her brusquely.

'I can't go to your friends' for lunch, Max,' she told him. 'Surely you can see why?'

He shook his head. 'No, I'm afraid I can't.'

'I knew Jill Trent quite well. She'll remember what – what happened.'

Max gave an impatient sigh. 'It happened to me too, you know. I was the one who had to stay and face the music, in case you've forgotten. If *I* don't mind, why should you?' When she didn't reply he grasped her shoulders and forced her to look at him. 'Bryony! We're *together* again – that's all that matters. It's inevitable that we'll come across people who remember what happened four years ago, but so what? It's none of their business. And after all, it was only a broken engagement. It was a nine days' wonder to most of them. Who do you think cares about it now, after all this time?'

Bryony bit her lip. *If only that was all it had been,* she cried out inwardly. If only it *was* just a nine days' wonder! Going back to St

Hildred's was out of the question. She knew there was just no way she could face it – not even for Max! 'I can't go!' she said. 'I *can't*. You go. I don't want to stop you seeing your friends.' She looked up at him pleadingly. 'Please, Max!'

His mouth tightened. 'All right. If that's your last word, I will go. It isn't what I'd planned for this weekend, Bryony, but it's your choice.'

'Perhaps we could go out somewhere this afternoon,' she called after him as he started back towards the house.

'Don't bank on it!' He turned to face her, his eyes dark with anger. 'I've never cared much for living in the past. You're like a ghost, Bryony – constantly haunting old ground, wringing your hands over past sorrows. Until you can forget them we're not going to get very far together, are we?'

Bryony stared at him helplessly, her eyes brimming with tears. If only there were something she could say – some way she could make him understand. For a moment they looked at each other, but Max's eyes remained angry and unyielding. He turned on his heel and went into the house.

She remained in the garden, hiding like a fugitive until the sound of a car engine starting and tyres on gravel told her that Max had left. To her relief the dining room was empty when she ventured back in through the open French windows. There was no one in the hall either, but as she put her foot on the bottom stair the study door opened and James Anderson came out.

'Bryony, will you come in here for a moment? I'd like to talk to you.'

She hesitated for a second, her hand on the banister rail, then resignedly she turned and followed him into the room. On his desk was a tray holding cups and a large pot of coffee. He nodded towards a chair. 'Do sit down. I thought you might like some coffee. Perhaps you'll pour for us.'

Bryony poured two cups and added cream and sugar, glad to have something with which to occupy her hands. As she passed Max's father his cup their eyes met and she caught her breath. In James Anderson's brown eyes there was a look of sympathy and compassion far beyond that of mere friend and doctor. What did he know? Before she could ask, he spoke:

'A pity you didn't go with Max to have lunch with Tony and Jill.' She could feel him looking at her, but she didn't meet his gaze, nor make any reply. He went on: 'I can't tell you how pleased I was to hear that you'd met again, Bryony. Perhaps I'm a sentimental old man, but I've been hoping that perhaps the two of you might get together again – permanently this time.' He sipped his coffee, regarding her over the rim of the cup. 'I daresay you've guessed that I plan to hand over the practice to Max when I retire in a couple of years' time? I'd like him to take my place as local police surgeon too, which is why he's doing this present course. Louise and I will be moving to a smaller house when I retire, and I've been nursing a fond picture of Max and you living here – producing a family of active grandchildren for me. I'd like that very much.'

Bryony smiled. 'Yes, it sounds wonderful, Dr Anderson.'

'Does it, Bryony? Is it what you'd like too?' He looked at her searchingly and she felt herself colouring.

'If you're asking what I *think* you're asking, Doctor, the answer is no.' She told him unhappily. 'It hasn't happened and I don't think it will – not now.'

He sighed and there was a long pause before he went on: 'Perhaps I should tell you about a case I was involved with recently,' he said quietly. 'In my capacity as police

226

surgeon, I mean.' He took a long draught of his coffee. 'We had a series of particularly nasty assaults,' he said. 'Sexual assaults. The man was finally caught and is now serving a long sentence, I'm happy to say.' He carefully refilled his cup from the coffee pot, then passed it to Bryony. 'It might have been hard to convict him but for one little self-indulgence he had. He kept a diary. It was found in his room after his arrest and the police were surprised to find that there'd been a good many unreported cases going back over a number of years. The diary contained detailed accounts of them all; descriptions of his victims, how he planned his attacks – where and when they took place, everything. It was as good as a signed confession.'

Bryony's mouth was too dry to speak as she stared at him.

'It seems that one of his victims was a young nurse from St Hildred's,' James went on gently. 'The date, the time, the description of the girl – it was all there, and it all fitted perfectly.' He put down his cup and leaned forward, his eyes earnest. 'It didn't take a genius to put two and two together. Why didn't you come to us, my dear? You must have thought us a cold-hearted bunch not to have been able to trust us.' He shook his head. 'It must have been a terrible ordeal for you.'

She nodded, her eyes afraid as they met his. 'No one can ever know, unless they've been through it too.' With an effort she met his eyes. 'You – never told anyone?'

He shook his head. 'There seemed little point. The man had been dealt with – you'd disappeared. There was no way it might have helped anyone.'

Bryony let out her breath on a long sigh. 'Thank God! Max doesn't know, you see. I could never tell him.'

His eyes were troubled. 'I have to say that I think you should, though. There'll be no true understanding between you until you do. That business this morning, for instance – I understood at once your reasons for not wanting to go.'

Bryony was silent, almost overwhelmed with despair. 'It would be over if I told him,' she whispered. 'He'd despise me. He'd be appalled – revolted.' Her shoulders slumped. 'Either way it seems there's no hope for us – for me.'

'I'm sure you're mistaken, my dear,' James told her kindly. 'It's impossible to predict another human being's reactions, of course, but I believe I know my own son.' He leaned forward towards her. 'Losing you went very deep with him, Bryony. I believe he cares a great deal for you.'

But Bryony had made up her mind. 'I must go,' she said, 'before Max gets back. I should never have come. It was a bad mistake, and I'm sure Max knows that too by now.' She rose to her feet. 'Will you drive me into Norwich, please? I'll catch a train from there. I hate to ask you on a Sunday, but...'

James was shaking his head. 'Oh, my dear, please reconsider. I meant to reassure you, not drive you away. Max will be so upset.'

'I don't think he will,' Bryony told him sadly. 'I think he knows as well as I do that it's not going to work after all. It's better this way – please?'

The elderly doctor sighed and stood up. 'If this is what you really feel is best, my dear, then of course I'll take you. I'm not happy about it, though. Not happy at all.'

As the train neared Bridgehurst station Bryony was faced with the difficult task of going back to the flat and explaining to Jane why she had returned. As she watched the depressingly dingy outer city landscape flashing by, bringing her nearer with every second, her heart sank. She felt unutterably weary of fabricated explanations and half truths. Suddenly she remembered something and opened her handbag, searching it frantically. Yes, there at the bottom was her salvation: the key to Alison's flat. It was empty and Alison had said she was welcome to use it. She would go there and spend the rest of the day in peace.

She took a taxi from the station and once inside Alison's flat she closed the door and breathed a sigh of relief. There was no food in the fridge, but she found dried milk and instant coffee in the cupboard and made herself a drink. She had no appetite anyway. But as she washed and dried her cup she realised that a whole afternoon and evening of her own company was abhorrent to her. Sitting at the window of the room that had once been hers, she suddenly thought of someone else who was alone; Peter Gardner. She would go and visit him. He at least would be pleased to have her company and perhaps seeing him would help put things into perspective for her.

The ward was full of Sunday afternoon visitors with their bunches of flowers, and bottles of fizzy glucose drink. Bryony stood for a moment in the entrance, wondering whether Peter was here or still in his side ward. The ward was so full of people that it was difficult to see. Then she caught sight of him in the bed at the end, looking heartachingly young and lonely, surrounded as he was by other people's chattering relatives.

He saw her and his eyes lit up with a surprised smile. She lifted her hand to wave and hurried towards him, laying the two paperbacks she had bought at the bookstall downstairs on his locker.

'Here, I hope you like these – I remembered how much you liked whodunits.' She smiled at him as she took off her coat and sat down. 'Well, how are you?'

'Great!' His eyes were bright. 'I had some good news this morning.'

'Really? What is it?'

'The X-rays show that the op was successful. There's every chance that I'll walk again.' He grinned. 'I was feeling a bit fed up, having no one to share it with, but now you're here!'

Bryony grasped his hand and pressed it warmly. 'Peter, that's wonderful! I'm so glad for you.'

'I'm to go to Stoke Mandeville for rehabilitation,' he hurried on excitedly. 'And the moment I can I'm going to apply for training as an occupational therapist.'

'You'll make it too, Peter. I know you will,' she told him.

'Yes, I will, because it's even more important now for me to prove myself.' Peter's eyes grew grave. 'I've learned a lot from all this,' he told her quietly. 'There was a time when I thought it was the end of the world, what happened to me, but lying here I've been taking stock.' He glanced at her. 'To begin with, look at all the friends I've made – people I'd never have met if it hadn't been for my illness; like you, for instance.' He smiled at her. 'Then there's this op. I see now that you should never miss a chance when it's offered – any chance, because I've realised that nothing that happens in life is without a reason. The trick is looking for that reason and learning from it, instead of feeling sorry for yourself and moaning about the rotten deal you've had.'

When the visitors' bell had rung Bryony left, promising to come again before Peter was transferred. Walking along the corridors on her way out of the hospital, she was deep in thought. Peter was right. He was still little more than a boy, yet he had learned what a good many people never learn in a lifetime. She felt proud of him – proud and ashamed at the same time. She herself could learn a lot from the things Peter had said this afternoon if only she had the courage.

'Hello there!'

She looked up as she walked out of the building, realising that someone was speaking to her.

'What are you doing here this afternoon?' Alison's social worker friend, Joan Medworth, fell into step beside her.

'I had some time to spare, so I popped in to visit a patient,' Bryony told her. 'Peter Gardner, one of Bill Kershore's paraplegics. He had an operation last week and he heard today that there's every chance he might walk again.'

Joan sighed. 'That's great. It's nice to hear some good news. I've had a pretty traumatic day myself. A patient who was discharged earlier last week was re-admitted this morning. She'd taken an overdose, I'm afraid. Your aunt would have been very upset and disappointed. I'm glad she's not here to see it.'

Bryony's blood chilled as a suspicion filled her mind. 'It's not – not *Glenys,* is it?' she whispered. 'She's not *dead?*'

Joan shook her head. 'It was touch and go. It seems that she heard on the radio that the man who attacked her has been caught. She was terrified that she'd have to go to court and give evidence – so the poor child took what she saw as the only way out. Luckily a neighbour found her in time. She's out of danger now, thank God.' She looked curiously at Bryony. 'Do you know her?'

'I've heard of the case from Alison. Wasn't she one of the first cases brought into the new VES?'

'That's right. Her physical injuries healed well, but...' Joan shook her head, 'her mental state is something else, as this has proved. She couldn't be persuaded to talk about it, you see. Not only did she refuse to report that she'd been raped, but she seemed to be trying to block it out – pretending it hadn't happened.' She shook her head. 'She was told on discharge that she could come back to the centre any time she felt she needed help, but the trouble is that as yet we have so few experienced counsellors we can call on. I don't think she really found the kind of help she needed here, which is sad.'

Bryony's heart was thudding in her chest.

Something deep inside told her that she was being offered *her* chance – the chance Peter had spoken of, that one couldn't afford to pass up. All the tangled and confused thoughts that had chased themselves through her mind continuously over the past four years seemed suddenly to weave themselves into a brilliantly clear pattern. She heard herself saying: 'Let me help. I was asked before, but somehow I – I never have.'

Joan looked doubtful and a little startled. 'Well, I don't know...'

'I *can* help,' Bryony urged. 'I have experience – personal experience. Alison tried her hardest to get me to volunteer, but I was too much of a coward. I see that now.'

'Wait a minute.' Joan laid a hand on Bryony's arm. 'Look, are you sure you want to do this?'

'Very sure,' Bryony told her.

Joan looked at her. 'Would you like to go now?'

Bryony's mouth was dry but her voice was firm as she answered: 'Yes, why not?'

CHAPTER ELEVEN

The girl lay in a small side ward, and Bryony went in alone. She was surprised at how small Glenys was; her body hardly made a mound under the bedclothes at all. Her face was to the wall and at first Bryony had no way of knowing whether or not she was asleep. Quietly she drew up a chair and sat down.

'Hello, Glenys,' she said. 'My name is Bryony.' Very gently she touched the thin hand lying on the coverlet. Glenys turned her head to look at her visitor with huge frightened blue eyes. She was little more than a child and she looked heart-wrenchingly young with her fragile little face and fair hair.

'I'd like you to tell me what happened to you, Glenys,' Bryony said softly. 'The truth, I mean.' She saw the look of alarm in the girl's eyes and added quickly, 'No, I'm not a policewoman – or anything else official, for that matter. I'm just someone who cares.' She leaned closer to the fragile figure. 'You see, it happened to me too, and I'm certain

237

that the only way to make the horror go away is to share it with someone. That's why I'm here.'

Glenys turned slightly to face her. 'It – happened to you?' she whispered incredulously. 'You mean *you* were – were…?'

'*Raped?*' Seeing the girl flinch, Bryony scarcely felt the stab of pain as the word pierced her own heart. 'It's an ugly word, isn't it?' she said. 'And an even uglier deed. It's brutal and despicable, but worse even than the physical hurt is the fact that it makes you feel *you're* to blame – that in some way you deserved it – just for being a woman. That feeling makes you feel angry and helpless and utterly alone, and because nobody seems to understand that, the whole horrible circle goes round and round in your head till you feel you're going crazy.' She pressed the thin hand that lay in her own and looked into the girl's eyes. 'I'm right, aren't I? That's why you're back here today?'

Glenys nodded wordlessly, tears squeezing out from under her lashes to slide down her cheeks.

Bryony swallowed hard. 'I'm going to tell you what happened to me now, Glenys,' she said, ignoring the sickening pounding of her heart. 'And then, if you feel you can, I want you to tell me your story. I've been going through hell for the last four years. I let it ruin my life. Even when people tried to show me the way, I wouldn't listen. I even threw away a second chance when I had it. But I know now where I went wrong, and even though it might be too late for me, I don't want that to happen to you.'

It was almost as though she was playing a tape that had been tightly coiled inside her mind – opening a locked box and letting the contents spill out. She talked, letting everything out – talked without a thought for how long. She told the girl in the bed details she had never disclosed to anyone, not even Alison. Glenys listened, her eyes brimming with tears, and when Bryony came to the end of her story she sat up and threw her arms around her.

'I didn't think anyone else could possibly have gone through what I did – or feel the same as me,' she sobbed. 'I felt I *couldn't* tell anyone, that if I did everyone would hate me – think me a liar. But now I know that you'll believe me.' Slowly and tearfully, she related her own story. By the time she had finished Bryony too was in tears. She held the girl tenderly, quietly weeping with her until at last Glenys drew away to lie back against the pillows again, exhausted but relaxed for the first time in weeks.

'Thank you for helping me,' she whispered. 'I feel so much better now.'

'I'm glad.' Bryony opened her handbag and scribbled her telephone number on the back of an old envelope. 'My address and phone number are here,' she said, pressing it into the girl's hand. 'After you leave here, please remember that there's always someone who'll listen at the other end of a telephone. If you're feeling bad again, any time – or even if you just want to talk, ring me, eh?' Glenys nodded and they exchanged a smile.

In the doorway Bryony paused as a thought occurred to her. 'Some time soon, when you're feeling a little better, will you do something for me, Glenys?'

The girl nodded eagerly. 'Of course – anything.'

'There's a young man called Peter Gardner in Men's Surgical,' Bryony said. 'He's just had a spinal operation to help him walk again after a severe mugging. He has no family. I have a feeling you might find you have a lot in common. Will you pop down and see him? I know he'd like that.'

'Of course I'll go,' promised Glenys. 'Tomorrow, if they let me get up.'

Bryony smiled. 'Good. 'Bye, then. Take care of yourself, Glenys.'

Outside in the corridor she stood for a moment, leaning against the wall, her eyes closed. She felt disorientated and a little dizzy. The interview with Glenys had drained her emotionally. But deep inside she felt cleansed and light, as though she had wakened from a nightmare to sunshine and a new day.

Slowly she walked to the lift, feeling as though her legs were made of lead. She longed for a drink of some kind – hot, strong tea, then four walls and a locked door – time to think through all that had happened. She reached out a hand to the lift button, but before she could press it the lift came into view and stopped. The doors opened and suddenly she found herself face to face with its only occupant – Max.

'Bryony! So you *are* here.' He took a step towards her.

For a moment she almost took to her heels and ran, but Max seemed to sense what was in her mind. Putting out a hand, he caught her wrist. 'Weren't you waiting for the lift?'

'Y-Yes, but...'

'Get in, then.'

Bryony complied resignedly, and he pressed the button for the ground floor. 'What are you doing here?' she asked him.

'Looking for you, mainly,' he told her crisply. 'I went to the flat and found no one at home, so I came on here.' She swayed dizzily as the lift came to a halt and Max shot out a hand to grasp her arm. His voice softened as he said: 'You look all in. Have you eaten anything since this morning at breakfast?'

She frowned, trying to remember. 'No, I don't think I have.'

He shook his head at her reprovingly. 'What are you trying to do – starve yourself to death? You'd better come with me and have something to eat before you pass out.'

She went with him without arguing, feeling unequal to protesting, or to asking the questions that buzzed confusedly in her mind.

In the visitors' cafeteria on the ground floor Max sat her down at one of the tables and stood looking down at her inquiringly. 'Well, what'll it be? Not that there's much choice at this hour. I daresay it's a case of beans on toast or – beans on toast!'

She shook her head. 'I'm not really

hungry. Anything will do, thank you.'

At this in-between time of the afternoon the canteen was almost empty and Bryony leaned back in her chair, watching helplessly as Max walked up to the counter and took a tray from the pile at the end. She felt trapped. All she had really wanted was to slip away back to Alison's flat where she could be by herself and think things out until they fell into some sort of shape. Yet there was no denying the feeling of strength and comfort Max's presence gave her as he placed the much needed food before her and urged her to eat.

'I managed to persuade them to make you an omelette – thought it might be slightly more tempting than the beans.'

She ate slowly and, after swallowing the first mouthful, found that she was hungry after all. Max watched without talking, leaning back in his chair, but once or twice she caught him looking at her in a way that made her heart quicken. He had the air of a man who was waiting – biding his time patiently. There was little doubt that he would demand an explanation from her once she had eaten. For the second time she had run out on him, and by the determined glint in his eye he wasn't going to let anything stop him from getting at the truth this time. Bryony took a long drink of the hot strong tea he had brought for her. Well, once he knew, he would probably wish he hadn't asked, she told herself bitterly.

But to her surprise he asked her nothing. When at last she laid down her knife and fork and pushed the empty cup to one side he stood up, holding out a hand to her. 'Shall we go?'

She bit her lip. 'Go – where?' she asked falteringly.

'Somewhere where you can rest for a while. You look exhausted.' Without another word he took her hand and led her out to the car park.

The drive lasted only minutes and Bryony was only slightly surprised to find that he was taking her to his flat. He stood aside for her to go up the stairs first, and it had occurred to her that he was taking no chances on her cutting and running. He must have read her thoughts; she certainly felt like it as the moment she was dreading drew closer.

Inside the flat it was quiet and peaceful, evening sunshine bathing the pleasant living room with golden light. The windows looked down on to a small park with grass and trees. Bryony stood for a moment watching some children playing with a ball, feeling oddly detached as though it was someone else who stood there and not Bryony Slade at all. The children's laughter reached her as she stood watching, shrill and excited. A dog had suddenly appeared from nowhere and taken possession of their ball, dribbling it crazily away from them across the grass with its nose. They shouted with merriment, falling over each other in their haste to scramble after it. Suddenly Bryony knew that she could tell Max – could say the things she had locked away. Perhaps talking to Glenys had broken the barriers, released her from the guilt and shame that had cruelly imprisoned her for the past four years.

'I've been talking to Glenys,' she said without turning round. 'The girl who overdosed this morning – the rape victim.' She turned then and her eyes looked straight into his, ready to face whatever she might see in them.

But Max's eyes looked back steadily into hers. 'I know,' he said. 'I ran into Joan Medworth and she told me where you were – what you'd offered to do. It was very good

245

of you.' He took a tentative step towards her. 'Why did you run away again, Bryony?' he asked, his voice quiet and low.

Bryony lifted her shoulders helplessly. 'For the same reason as before. Max, there's something I have to say to you – to tell you about. It's about what happened four years ago. I realise that what I did must have hurt you very much. It must have seemed a terrible, heartless – unforgivable thing to do. I'm afraid at the time I didn't think very much about the consequences for you. All I knew was that you were better off without me – that you wouldn't want me when you knew...' Her voice caught in the tightness of her throat. She shook her head. *Surely she wasn't going to cry again?* She had been so sure that she had the courage to do this! She fought to control the surge of emotion that threatened to let her down. 'I'm not looking for sympathy, Max, please believe that. What happened was...'

But he had seen the hands clenching into tight fists at her sides, the way her pale cheeks had drained of what little colour they had. He had tried to let her tell it her own way because he knew it was important for her, but he couldn't bear to stand there and watch her struggling for control any longer.

He closed the distance between them in one stride and took both of her hands in his. 'No more, Bryony. That's enough. You don't have to go on. I *know*. Dad told me – this afternoon, after you'd left,' he told her huskily. 'He asked me to beg your forgiveness for breaking your confidence, but he felt it was the only way. He knew I'd want to know. He also felt fairly certain you'd never tell me.' He let go of her hands and caught her shoulders, pulling her towards him, his voice ragged as he said: '*Why* couldn't you have come to me before, Bryony?' His eyes searched hers and his fingers bit deeply into her shoulders. 'For God's sake, have you any idea how it feels to know you inspire so little trust or faith? *Why* did you run away from me like that? Did I really seem so shallow and superficial to you?' His eyes were clouded as he went on: 'Not knowing why you'd gone was such hell! I lay awake night after night, racking my brain – asking myself where I'd gone wrong, how I'd failed you.'

She shook her head. 'No! It was more that I felt *I'd* failed *you*,' she whispered. 'I couldn't bear the thought of *anyone* knowing, Max – couldn't even talk about it; and the thought of your horror and disgust – the revulsion I knew you'd feel.'

Max was shaking his head in disbelief. 'God, you couldn't really have thought I'd react like that! Did you, Bryony? *Did you?*'

Bryony bit her lip. 'I don't know what I thought. At the time everything looked so black. I just wanted to run away and hide – pretend it hadn't happened – start again in some place where no one knew.' She forced herself to look up at him. 'As for you – *us;* things hadn't been working out too well. I felt I'd already disappointed you and that it would have been unfair to put our relationship to that kind of test. I reasoned that perhaps I'd never been right for you anyway.' She sighed, suddenly feeling almost unbearably weary. 'Then, when we met again – when it looked as though there might just be a chance for us after all...' She shrugged. 'This weekend started so well. I'd really begun to let myself believe that everything might possibly work out after all. Then this morning it all came home to me again just as it always does – being invited to the hospital for lunch, knowing I couldn't face the thought of going there, meeting people from the past.' She turned away from him despairingly. 'It's like having a criminal record, Max. It always catches up with you, however hard you try to put it behind you. I

248

realised that the barriers would always be there between us and I knew then that I had to make a choice: either I had to tell you the truth and see you turn away from me – or get out again. This time for good.' She looked at him. 'You know what I chose – in spite of your father's kindness.' She shrugged helplessly, blinking hard as tears blurred her vision. 'Don't think I haven't despised myself for the coward I am. That was why I had to make myself go and see that poor girl this afternoon. I should have done it weeks ago, as Alison asked me. I knew I could help her if only I had the guts to do it, and I think I was able to reach her, thank God.'

Max lifted her chin to look into her eyes. 'And *me*, Bryony? Are you going to let me reach *you?*'

Her eyes held his candidly. 'Do you really want to, Max – now that you know?' she whispered. 'And I *mean* really – because the time for reassuring sympathy was over long ago.'

For a long moment he looked into her eyes, his own dark with a mixture of emotions she daren't let herself try to read. 'Do you really have to ask that question, Bryony?' He drew her close, looking down at her. 'All I ask is that you let me try to show you how much I want to – how much you mean to me.'

She frowned. 'It might not be easy, Max. We can't just pick up where we left off. That's one of the things that became clear to me this morning. I'm a different person now, after four years – after what happened. Before, I had such high ideals. I wanted everything to be perfect. Now I know it can never be that.'

He raised her chin to search her eyes again. 'Do you think it left *me* unscathed, Bryony?' he asked her. 'Do you think *I* haven't changed too? Looking back now, I understand so many things that puzzled me before. I feel angry with myself for the insensitive brute I must have seemed – and angry with *you* for not putting me wise.' His eyes searched hers. 'As for wanting everything to be perfect, Bryony – that was always an illusion. We live in a far from perfect world. But that's not to say we can't try to make our own perfection with what we have.' Very gently he kissed her. 'The important thing is – do you love me?'

Bryony nodded, her mouth dry. 'I never stopped loving you,' she told him. 'Never for one moment. Don't you see, that's what hurt so much – so very, *very* much. And last night, I wanted so desperately to explain – when I couldn't – when you...'

Her lips were trembling as he stopped her words with a kiss. His lips captured hers tenderly till he felt the tension go out of her body and she relaxed against him, eyes closed, her arms clinging to him.

'Shall I tell you what's going to happen?' he asked her after a little while. 'We're going to be married just as soon as we can arrange it.' He rocked her gently in his arms, his chin resting on top of her head. 'Then at the end of my course we're going home to Arden House to start that new life together. Who knows – maybe after a year or two we'll even get around to starting that family of "active grandchildren" Dad sets such store by!' He looked down at her and this time his eyes were smiling. 'How's that for perfection, Bryony? Perfection Anderson style?'

She slipped her arms around his waist, underneath his jacket, pressing her face against his chest, grateful for the comforting warmth of his skin against her cheek and the strength of his arms holding her tightly. 'It sounds almost too beautiful to be true,' she told him happily.

He kissed her deeply, then cupped her

chin to look into her eyes. 'First there's something else,' he said softly. 'Something I think you know is very important for both of us. Last night, before any of this came out, I spoke about having some time to ourselves – time to rediscover each other, because I sensed even then that we still had a barrier to break. Let's make that time now, Bryony. We only have until tomorrow morning, but I have a feeling it's enough.' He looked deep into her eyes. 'I love you very much, darling. Can you trust me to make the memories go away – or at least to try?'

The look in his eyes told her all she wanted to know, promised all she'd ever dreamed of, and her heart was so full of her love for him that she could only nod and cling to him as he lifted her in his arms.

Bryony woke at first light and lay for a moment, letting the first rays of light play on her closed eyelids. Last night had been like a revelation; like the true beginning of her new life. Although she had tried not to let Max see, she had been tense and fearful at first, but he had lovingly soothed her fears away. He had been so gentle and patient with her, coaxing her fears away, erasing all the bad memories for ever; sweetly arousing

252

her senses until she went to him eagerly and longingly. Afterwards she had lain in his arms and wept tears of pure joy, thanking heaven for another chance – and for giving Max back to her.

She turned her head to look at him, still sleeping beside her. The tension had disappeared from his face, softening the lines around his mouth and eyes, so that he looked as he had when they had first met. They would be married as soon as possible, in the little village church at East Keel, just as they were to have been four years ago. They had planned it all last night, lying happily in each other's arms just before they had fallen asleep. But Bryony had known then that in fact they belonged to each other already. The real beginning of their new life together had begun last night, when the past had been erased at last and she had gone into his arms freely and joyfully. Nothing in the world could ever change that now. The thought filled her with an almost overwhelming happiness.

She reached out a finger to trace the line of his jaw, feeling the roughness of his beard grating under her fingertip. He opened his eyes to meet hers with his warm, wonderful smile.

'Good morning,' he said drowsily, drawing her into the crook of his arm. 'Good morning – Mrs Anderson.'

She kissed him softly. 'It's more than just a good morning, darling. It's a wonderful, *special* morning,' she told him. 'The very best I ever wakened to.'

The publishers hope that this book has given you enjoyable reading. Large Print Books are especially designed to be as easy to see and hold as possible. If you wish a complete list of our books please ask at your local library or write directly to:

Dales Large Print Books
Magna House, Long Preston,
Skipton, North Yorkshire.
BD23 4ND

This Large Print Book, for people
who cannot read normal print,
is published under the auspices of

THE ULVERSCROFT FOUNDATION